THE NOTEBOOK

THE NOTEBOOK

Nicholas Sparks

WARNER BOOKS

A Time Warner Company

This book is a work of fiction. Names, characters, places and inci-
dents are either the product of the author's imagination or are used
fictitiously, and any resemblance to actual persons, living or dead,
events, or locales is entirely coincidental.

Warner Books, Inc., 1271 Avenue of the Americas, New York, NY
10020

 A Time Warner Company

Printed in the United States of America
First Printing: October 1996
10   9   8   7

Library of Congress Cataloging-in-Publication Data

Sparks, Nicholas.
    The notebook / Nicholas Sparks.
        p.   cm.
    ISBN 0-446-52080-2
    1. Man-woman relationships—North Carolina—Fiction.
2. Oral reading—Fiction. 3. Aged—Fiction. I. Title.
PS3569.P363N68   1996
813'.54—dc20   96-33815
                                                   CIP

Book design and composition by L & G McRee

This book is dedicated with love to
Cathy,
my wife and my friend.

Acknowledgments

This story is what it is today because of two special people, and I would like to thank them for everything they've done.

To Theresa Park, the agent who plucked me from obscurity. Thank you for your kindness, your patience, and the many hours you have spent working with me. I will be forever grateful for everything you've done.

To Jamie Raab, my editor. Thank you for your wisdom, your humor, and your good-hearted nature. You made this a wonderful experience for me, and I'm glad to call you my friend.

THE NOTEBOOK

Miracles

W
ho am I? And how, I wonder, will this story end?

The sun has come up and I am sitting by a window that is foggy with the breath of a life gone by. I'm a sight this morning: two shirts, heavy pants, a scarf wrapped twice around my neck and tucked into a thick sweater knitted by my daughter thirty birthdays ago. The thermostat in my room is set as high as it will go, and a smaller space heater sits directly behind me. It clicks and groans and spews hot air like a fairy-tale dragon, and still my body shivers with a cold that will never go away, a cold that has been eighty years in the making. Eighty years, I think sometimes, and despite my own acceptance of my age, it still amazes me that I haven't been warm since George Bush was president.

I wonder if this is how it is for everyone my age.

My life? It isn't easy to explain. It has not been the rip-roaring spectacular I fancied it would be, but neither have I burrowed around with the gophers. I suppose it has most resembled a blue-chip stock: fairly stable, more ups than downs, and gradually trending upward over time. A good buy, a lucky buy, and I've learned that not everyone can say this about his life. But do not be misled. I am nothing special; of this I am sure. I am a common man with common thoughts, and I've led a common life. There are no monuments dedicated to me and my name will soon be forgotten, but I've loved another with all my heart and soul, and to me, this has always been enough.

The romantics would call this a love story, the cynics would call it a tragedy. In my mind it's a little bit of both, and no matter how you choose to view it in the end, it does not change the fact that it involves a great deal of my life and the path I've chosen to follow. I have no complaints about my path and the places it has taken me; enough complaints to fill a circus tent about other things, maybe, but the path I've chosen has always been the right one, and I wouldn't have had it any other way.

Time, unfortunately, doesn't make it easy to stay on course. The path is straight as ever, but now it is strewn with the rocks and gravel that accumulate over a lifetime. Until three years ago it would have been easy to ignore, but it's impossible now. There is a sickness rolling through my body; I'm neither strong nor healthy, and my days are spent like an old party balloon: listless, spongy, and growing softer over time.

I cough, and through squinted eyes I check my watch. I realize it is time to go. I stand from my seat by the window and shuffle across the room, stopping at the desk to pick up the notebook I have read a hundred times. I do not glance through it. Instead I slip it beneath my arm and continue on my way to the place I must go.

I walk on tiled floors, white in color and speckled with gray. Like my hair and the hair of most people here, though I'm the only one in the hallway this morning. They are in their rooms, alone except for television, but they, like me, are used to it. A person can get used to anything, if given enough time.

I hear the muffled sounds of crying in the distance and know exactly who is making those sounds. Then the nurses see me and we smile at each other and exchange greetings. They are my friends and we talk often, but I am sure they wonder about me and the things that I go through every day. I listen as they begin to whisper among themselves as I pass. "There he goes again," I hear, "I hope it turns out well." But they say nothing directly to me about it. I'm sure they think it would hurt me to talk about it so early in the morning, and knowing myself as I do, I think they're probably right.

A minute later, I reach the room. The door has been propped open for me, as it usually is. There are two others in the room, and they too smile at me as I enter. "Good morning," they say with cheery voices, and I take a moment to ask about the kids and the schools and upcoming vacations. We talk above the crying for a minute or so. They do not seem to notice; they have become numb to it, but then again, so have I.

Afterward I sit in the chair that has come to be shaped like me. They are finishing up now; her clothes are on, but still she is crying. It will become quieter after they leave, I know. The excitement of the morning always upsets her, and today is no exception. Finally the shade is opened and the nurses walk out. Both of them touch me and smile as they walk by. I wonder what this means.

I sit for just a second and stare at her, but she doesn't return the look. I understand, for she doesn't know who I am. I'm a stranger to her. Then, turning away, I bow my head and pray silently for the strength I know I will need. I have always been a firm believer in God and the power of prayer, though to be honest, my faith has made for a list of questions I definitely want answered after I'm gone.

Ready now. On go the glasses, out of my pocket comes a magnifier. I put it on the table for a moment while I open the notebook. It takes two licks on my gnarled finger to get the well-worn cover open to the first page. Then I put the magnifier in place.

There is always a moment right before I begin to read the story when my mind churns, and I wonder, Will it happen today? I don't know, for I never know beforehand, and deep down it really doesn't matter. It's the possibility that keeps me going, not the guarantee, a sort of wager on my part. And though you may call me a dreamer or fool or any other thing, I believe that anything is possible.

I realize the odds, and science, are against me. But science is not the total answer; this I know, this I have learned in my lifetime. And that leaves me with the belief that miracles, no matter how inexplicable or unbelievable, are real and can occur without regard to the natural order of things. So once again, just as I do every day, I begin to read the notebook aloud, so that she can hear it, in the hope that the miracle that has come to dominate my life will once again prevail.

And maybe, just maybe, it will.

Ghosts

It was early October 1946, and Noah Calhoun watched the fading sun sink lower from the wraparound porch of his plantation-style home. He liked to sit here in the evenings, especially after working hard all day, and let his thoughts wander without conscious direction. It was how he relaxed, a routine he'd learned from his father.

He especially liked to look at the trees and their reflections in the river. North Carolina trees are beautiful in deep autumn: greens, yellows, reds, oranges, every shade in between. Their dazzling colors glow with the sun, and for the hundredth time, Noah Calhoun wondered if the original owners of the house had spent their evenings thinking the same things.

 The house was built in 1772, making it one of

the oldest, as well as largest, homes in New Bern. Originally it was the main house on a working plantation, and he had bought it right after the war ended and had spent the last eleven months and a small fortune repairing it. The reporter from the Raleigh paper had done an article on it a few weeks ago and said it was one of the finest restorations he'd ever seen. At least the house was. The remaining property was another story, and that was where he'd spent most of the day.

The home sat on twelve acres adjacent to Brices Creek, and he'd worked on the wooden fence that lined the other three sides of the property, checking for dry rot or termites, replacing posts when he had to. He still had more work to do on it, especially on the west side, and as he'd put the tools away earlier he'd made a mental note to call and have some more lumber delivered. He'd gone into the house, drunk a glass of sweet tea, then showered. He always showered at the end of the day, the water washing away both dirt and fatigue.

Afterward he'd combed his hair back, put on some faded jeans and a long-sleeved blue shirt, poured himself another glass of sweet tea, and gone to the porch, where he now sat, where he sat every day at this time.

He stretched his arms above his head, then out to the sides, rolling his shoulders as he completed the routine. He felt good and clean now, fresh. His muscles were tired and he knew he'd be a little sore tomorrow, but he was pleased that he had accomplished most of what he had wanted to do.

Noah reached for his guitar, remembering his father as he did so, thinking how much he missed him. He strummed once, adjusted the tension on two strings, then strummed again. This time it sounded about right, and he began to play. Soft music, quiet music. He hummed for a little while at first, then began to sing as night came down around him. He played and sang until the sun was gone and the sky was black.

It was a little after seven when he quit, and he settled back into his chair and began to rock. By habit, he looked upward and saw Orion and the Big Dipper, Gemini and the Pole Star, twinkling in the autumn sky.

He started to run the numbers in his head, then stopped. He knew he'd spent almost his entire savings on the house and would have to find a job again soon, but he pushed the thought away and decided to enjoy the remaining months of restoration without worrying about it. It would work out for him, he knew; it always did. Besides, thinking about money usually bored him. Early on, he'd learned to enjoy simple things, things that couldn't be bought, and he had a hard time understanding people who felt otherwise. It was another trait he got from his father.

Clem, his hound dog, came up to him then

and nuzzled his hand before lying down at his feet. "Hey, girl, how're you doing?" he asked as he patted her head, and she whined softly, her soft round eyes peering upward. A car accident had taken her leg, but she still moved well enough and kept him company on quiet nights like these.

He was thirty-one now, not too old, but old enough to be lonely. He hadn't dated since he'd been back here, hadn't met anyone who remotely interested him. It was his own fault, he knew. There was something that kept a distance between him and any woman who started to get close, something he wasn't sure he could change even if he tried. And sometimes in the moments right before sleep came, he wondered if he was destined to be alone forever.

The evening passed, staying warm, nice. Noah listened to the crickets and the rustling leaves, thinking that the sound of nature was more real and aroused more emotion than things like cars and planes. Natural things gave back more than they took, and their sounds always brought him back to the way man was supposed to be. There were times during the war, especially after a major engagement, when he had often thought about these simple sounds. "It'll keep you from going crazy," his father had told him the day he'd shipped out. "It's God's music and it'll take you home."

He finished his tea, went inside, found a book,

then turned on the porch light on his way back out. After sitting down again, he looked at the book. It was old, the cover was torn, and the pages were stained with mud and water. It was *Leaves of Grass* by Walt Whitman, and he had carried it with him throughout the war. It had even taken a bullet for him once.

He rubbed the cover, dusting it off just a little. Then he let the book open randomly and read the words in front of him:

> This is thy hour O Soul, thy free flight
>   into the wordless,
> Away from books, away from art, the day
>   erased, the lesson done,
> Thee fully forth emerging, silent, gazing,
>   pondering the themes thou lovest best,
> Night, sleep, death and the stars.

He smiled to himself. For some reason Whitman always reminded him of New Bern, and he was glad he'd come back. Though he'd been away for fourteen years, this was home and he knew a lot of people here, most of them from his youth. It wasn't surprising. Like so many southern towns, the people who lived here never changed, they just grew a bit older.

His best friend these days was Gus, a seventy-year-old black man who lived down the road. They had met a couple of weeks after Noah bought the house, when Gus had shown up with some homemade liquor and Brunswick stew, and the two had spent their first evening together getting drunk and telling stories.

Now Gus would show up a couple of nights a week, usually around eight. With four kids and eleven grandchildren in the house, he needed to get out of the house now and then, and Noah couldn't blame him. Usually Gus would bring his harmonica, and after talking for a little while, they'd play a few songs together. Sometimes they played for hours.

He'd come to regard Gus as family. There really wasn't anyone else, at least not since his father died last year. He was an only child; his mother had died of influenza when he was two, and though he had wanted to at one time, he had never married.

But he had been in love once, that he knew. Once and only once, and a long time ago. And it had changed him forever. Perfect love did that to a person, and this had been perfect.

Coastal clouds slowly began to roll across the evening sky, turning silver with the reflection of the moon. As they thickened, he leaned his head back and rested it against the rocking chair. His legs moved automatically, keeping a steady rhythm, and as he did most evenings, he felt his mind drifting back to a warm evening like this fourteen years ago.

It was just after graduation 1932, the opening night of the Neuse River Festival. The town was out in full, enjoying barbecue and games of chance. It was humid that night—for some reason he remembered that clearly. He arrived alone, and as he strolled through the crowd, looking for friends, he saw Fin and Sarah, two people he'd grown up with, talking to a girl he'd never seen before. She was pretty, he remembered thinking, and when he finally joined them, she looked his way with a pair of hazy eyes that kept on coming. "Hi," she'd said simply as she offered her hand, "Finley's told me a lot about you."

An ordinary beginning, something that would have been forgotten had it been anyone but her. But as he shook her hand and met those striking emerald eyes, he knew before he'd taken his next breath that she was the one he could spend the rest of his life looking for but never find again. She seemed that good, that perfect, while a summer wind blew through the trees.

From there, it went like a tornado wind. Fin told him she was spending the summer in New Bern with her family because her father worked for R. J. Reynolds, and though he only nodded, the way she was looking at him made his silence seem okay. Fin laughed then, because he knew what was happening, and Sarah suggested they get some cherry Cokes, and the four of them stayed at the festival until the crowds were thin and everything closed up for the night.

They met the following day, and the day after

that, and they soon became inseparable. Every morning but Sunday when he had to go to church, he would finish his chores as quickly as possible, then make a straight line to Fort Totten Park, where she'd be waiting for him. Because she was a newcomer and hadn't spent time in a small town before, they spent their days doing things that were completely new to her. He taught her how to bait a line and fish the shallows for largemouth bass and took her exploring through the backwoods of the Croatan Forest. They rode in canoes and watched summer thunderstorms, and to him it seemed as though they'd always known each other.

But he learned things as well. At the town dance in the tobacco barn, it was she who taught him how to waltz and do the Charleston, and though they stumbled through the first few songs, her patience with him eventually paid off, and they danced together until the music ended. He walked her home afterward, and when they paused on the porch after saying good night, he kissed her for the first time and wondered why he had waited as long as he had. Later in the summer he brought her to this house, looked past the decay, and told her that one day he was going to own it and fix it up. They spent hours together talking about their dreams—his of seeing the world, hers of being an artist—and on a humid night in August, they both lost their virginity. When she left three weeks later, she took a piece of him and the rest of summer with her. He watched her leave town on an early rainy morning, watched through eyes that hadn't slept the night before, then went home and packed a bag. He spent the next week alone on Harkers Island.

Noah ran his hands through his hair and checked his watch. Eight-twelve. He got up and walked to the front of the house and looked up the road. Gus wasn't in sight, and Noah figured he wouldn't be coming. He went back to his rocker and sat again.

He remembered talking to Gus about her. The first time he mentioned her, Gus started to shake his head and laugh. "So that's the ghost you been running from." When asked what he meant, Gus said, "You know, the ghost, the memory. I been watchin' you, workin' day and night, slavin' so hard you barely have time to catch your breath. People do that for three reasons. Either they crazy, or stupid, or tryin' to forget. And with you, I knew you was tryin' to forget. I just didn't know what."

He thought about what Gus had said. Gus was right, of course. New Bern was haunted now. Haunted by the ghost of her memory. He saw her in Fort Totten Park, their place, every time he walked by. Either sitting on the bench or standing by the gate, always smiling, blond hair softly touching her shoulders, her eyes the color of emeralds. When he sat on the porch at night with his guitar, he saw her beside him, listening quietly as he played the music of his childhood.

He felt the same when he went to Gaston's Drug Store, or to the Masonic theater, or even when he strolled downtown. Everywhere he looked, he saw her image, saw things that brought her back to life.

It was odd, he knew that. He had grown up in New Bern. Spent his first seventeen years here. But when he thought about New Bern, he seemed to remember only the last summer, the summer they were together. Other memories were simply fragments, pieces here and there of growing up, and few, if any, evoked any feeling.

He had told Gus about it one night, and not only had Gus understood, but he had been the first to explain why. He said simply, "My daddy used to tell me that the first time you fall in love, it changes your life forever, and no matter how hard you try, the feelin' never goes away. This girl you been tellin' me about was your first love. And no matter what you do, she'll stay with you forever."

Noah shook his head, and when her image began to fade, he returned to Whitman. He read for an hour, looking up every now and then to see raccoons and possums scurrying near the creek. At nine-thirty he closed the book, went upstairs to the bedroom, and wrote in his journal, including both personal observations and the work he'd accomplished on the house. Forty minutes later, he was sleeping. Clem wandered up the stairs, sniffed him as he slept, and then paced in circles before finally curling up at the foot of his bed.

Earlier that evening and a hundred miles away, she sat alone on the porch swing of her parents' home, one leg crossed beneath her. The seat had been slightly damp when she sat down; rain had fallen earlier, hard and stinging, but the clouds were fading now and she looked past them, toward the stars, wondering if she'd made the right decision. She'd struggled with it for days—and had struggled some more this evening—but in the end, she knew she would never forgive herself if she let the opportunity slip away.

Lon didn't know the real reason she left the following morning. The week before, she'd hint-ed to him that she might want to visit some antique shops near the coast. "It's just a couple of days," she said, "and besides, I need a break from planning the wedding." She felt bad about the lie but knew there was no way she could tell him the truth. Her leaving had nothing to do with him, and it wouldn't be fair of her to ask him to understand.

It was an easy drive from Raleigh, slightly more than two hours, and she arrived a little before eleven. She checked into a small inn downtown, went to her room, and unpacked her suitcase, hanging her dresses in the closet and putting everything else in the drawers. She had a quick lunch, asked the waitress for directions to the nearest antique stores, then spent the next few hours shopping. By four-thirty she was back in her room.

She sat on the edge of the bed, picked up the phone, and called Lon. He couldn't speak long, he was due in court, but before they hung up she gave him the phone number where she was staying and promised to call the following day. Good, she thought while hanging up the phone. Routine conversation, nothing out of the ordinary. Nothing to make him suspicious.

She'd known him almost four years now; it was 1942 when they met, the world at war and America one year in. Everyone was doing their part, and she was volunteering at the hospital downtown. She was both needed and appreciated there, but it was more difficult than she'd expected. The first waves of wounded young soldiers were coming home, and she spent her days with broken men and shattered bodies. When Lon, with all his easy charm, introduced himself at a Christmas party, she saw in him exactly what she needed: someone with confidence about the future and a sense of humor that drove all her fears away.

He was handsome, intelligent, and driven, a successful lawyer eight years older than she, and he pursued his job with passion, not only winning cases, but also making a name for himself. She understood his vigorous pursuit of success, for her father and most of the men she met in her social circle were the same way. Like them, he'd been raised that way, and in the caste system of the South, family name and accomplishments were often the most important consideration in marriage. In some cases, they were the only consideration.

Though she had quietly rebelled against this idea since childhood and had dated a few men best described as reckless, she found herself drawn to Lon's easy ways and had gradually come to love him. Despite the long hours he worked, he was good to her. He was a gentleman, both mature and responsible, and during those terrible periods of the war when she needed someone to hold her, he never once turned her away. She felt secure with him and knew he loved her as well, and that was why she had accepted his proposal.

Thinking these things made her feel guilty about being here, and she knew she should pack her things and leave before she changed her mind. She had done it once before, long ago, and if she left now, she was sure she would never have the strength to return here again. She picked up her pocketbook, hesitated, and almost made it to the door. But coincidence had pushed her here, and she put the pocketbook down, again realizing that if she quit now, she would always wonder what would have happened. And she didn't think she could live with that.

She went to the bathroom and started a bath. After checking the temperature, she walked to the dresser, taking off her gold earrings as she crossed the room. She found her makeup bag, opened it, and pulled out a razor and a bar of soap, then undressed in front of the bureau.

She had been called beautiful since she was a young girl, and once she was naked, she looked at herself in the mirror. Her body was firm and well proportioned, breasts softly rounded, stomach flat, legs slim. She'd inherited her mother's high cheekbones, smooth skin, and blond hair, but her best feature was her own. She had "eyes like ocean waves," as Lon liked to say.

Taking the razor and soap, she went to the bathroom again, turned off the faucet, set a towel where she could reach it, and stepped in gingerly.

She liked the way a bath relaxed her, and she slipped lower in the water. The day had been long and her back was tense, but she was pleased she had finished shopping so quickly. She had to go back to Raleigh with something tangible, and the things she had picked out would work fine. She made a mental note to find the names of some other stores in the Beaufort area, then suddenly doubted she would need to. Lon wasn't the type to check up on her.

She reached for the soap, lathered up, and

began to shave her legs. As she did, she thought about her parents and what they would think of her behavior. No doubt they would disapprove, especially her mother. Her mother had never really accepted what had happened the summer they'd spent here and wouldn't accept it now, no matter what reason she gave.

She soaked a while longer in the tub before finally getting out and toweling off. She went to the closet and looked for a dress, finally choosing a long yellow one that dipped slightly in the front, the kind of dress that was common in the South. She slipped it on and looked in the mirror, turning from side to side. It fit her well and made her look feminine, but she eventually decided against it and put it back on the hanger.

Instead she found a more casual, less revealing dress and put that on. Light blue with a touch of lace, it buttoned up the front, and though it didn't look quite as nice as the first one, it conveyed an image she thought would be more appropriate.

She wore little makeup, just a touch of eye shadow and mascara to accent her eyes. Perfume next, not too much. She found a pair of small-hooped earrings, put those on, then slipped on the tan, low-heeled sandals she had been wearing earlier. She brushed her blond hair, pinned it up, and looked in the mirror. No, it was too much, she thought, and she let it back down. Better.

When she was finished she stepped back and

evaluated herself. She looked good: not too dressy, not too casual. She didn't want to overdo it. After all, she didn't know what to expect. It had been a long time—probably too long—and many different things could have happened, even things she didn't want to consider.

She looked down and saw her hands were shaking, and she laughed to herself. It was strange; she wasn't normally this nervous. Like Lon, she had always been confident, even as a child. She remembered that it had been a problem at times, especially when she dated, because it had intimidated most of the boys her age.

She found her pocketbook and car keys, then picked up the room key. She turned it over in her hand a couple of times, thinking, You've come this far, don't give up now, and almost left then, but instead sat on the bed again. She checked her watch. Almost six o'clock. She knew she had to leave in a few minutes—she didn't want to arrive after dark, but she needed a little more time.

"Damn," she whispered, "what am I doing here? I shouldn't be here. There's no reason for it," but once she said it she knew it wasn't true. There was something here. If nothing else, she would have her answer.

She opened her pocketbook and thumbed through it until she came to a folded-up piece of newspaper. After taking it out slowly, almost reverently, being careful not to rip it, she unfolded it and stared at it for a while. "This is why," she finally said to herself, "this is what it's all about."

Noah got up at five and kayaked for an hour up Brices Creek, as he usually did. When he finished, he changed into his work clothes, warmed some biscuits from the day before, grabbed a couple of apples, and washed his breakfast down with two cups of coffee.

He worked on the fencing again, repairing most of the posts that needed it. It was Indian summer, the temperature over eighty degrees, and by lunchtime he was hot and tired and glad for the break.

He ate at the creek because the mullets were jumping. He liked to watch them jump three or four times and glide through the air before vanishing into the brackish water. For some reason he had always been pleased by the fact that their instinct hadn't changed for thousands, maybe tens of thousands, of years.

Sometimes he wondered if man's instincts had changed in that time and always concluded that they hadn't. At least in the basic, most primal ways. As far as he could tell, man had always been aggressive, always striving to dominate, trying to control the world and everything in it. The war in Europe and Japan proved that.

He quit working a little after three and walked to a small shed that sat near his dock. He went in, found his fishing pole, a couple of lures, and some live crickets he kept on hand, then walked out to the dock, baited his hook, and cast his line.

Fishing always made him reflect on his life, and he did it now. After his mother died, he could remember spending his days in a dozen different homes, and for one reason or another, he stuttered badly as a child and was teased for it. He began to speak less and less, and by the age of five, he wouldn't speak at all. When he started classes, his teachers thought he was retarded and recommended that he be pulled out of school.

Instead, his father took matters into his own hands. He kept him in school and afterward made him come to the lumberyard, where he worked, to haul and stack wood. "It's good that we spend some time together," he would say as they worked side by side, "just like my daddy and I did."

During their time together, his father would talk about birds and animals or tell stories and legends common to North Carolina. Within a few months Noah was speaking again, though not well, and his father decided to teach him to read with books of poetry. "Learn to read this aloud and you'll be able to say anything you want to." His father had been right again, and by the following year, Noah had lost his stutter. But he continued to go to the lumberyard every day simply because his father was there, and in the evenings he would read the works of Whitman and Tennyson aloud as his father rocked beside him. He had been reading poetry ever since.

When he got a little older, he spent most of his weekends and vacations alone. He explored the Croatan Forest in his first canoe, following Brices Creek for twenty miles until he could go no farther, then hiked the remaining miles to the coast. Camping and exploring became his passion, and he spent hours in the forest, sitting beneath blackjack oak trees, whistling quietly, and playing his guitar for beavers and geese and wild blue herons. Poets knew that isolation in nature, far from people and things man-made, was good for the soul, and he'd always identified with poets.

Although he was quiet, years of heavy lifting at the lumberyard helped him excel in sports, and his athletic success led to popularity. He enjoyed the football games and track meets, and though most of his teammates spent their free time together as well, he rarely joined them. An occasional person found him arrogant; most simply figured he had grown up a bit faster than everyone else. He had a few girlfriends in school, but none had ever made an impression on him. Except for one. And she came after graduation.

Allie. His Allie.

He remembered talking to Fin about Allie after they'd left the festival that first night, and

Fin had laughed. Then he'd made two predictions: first, that they would fall in love, and second, that it wouldn't work out.

There was a slight tug at his line and Noah hoped for a largemouth bass, but the tugging eventually stopped, and after reeling his line in and checking the bait, he cast again.

Fin ended up being right on both counts. Most of the summer, she had to make excuses to her parents whenever they wanted to see each other. It wasn't that they didn't like him—it was that he was from a different class, too poor, and they would never approve if their daughter became serious with someone like him. "I don't care what my parents think, I love you and always will," she would say. "We'll find a way to be together."

But in the end they couldn't. By early September the tobacco had been harvested and she had no choice but to return with her family to Winston-Salem. "Only the summer is over, Allie, not us," he'd said the morning she left. "We'll never be over." But they were. For a reason he didn't fully understand, the letters he wrote went unanswered.

Eventually he decided to leave New Bern to help get her off his mind, but also because the Depression made earning a living in New Bern almost impossible. He went first to Norfolk and worked at a shipyard for six months before he was laid off, then moved to New Jersey because he'd heard the economy wasn't so bad there.

He eventually found a job in a scrap yard, separating scrap metal from everything else. The owner, a Jewish man named Morris Goldman, was intent on collecting as much scrap metal as he could, convinced that a war was going to start in Europe and that America would be dragged in again. Noah, though, didn't care about the reason. He was just happy to have a job.

His years in the lumberyard had toughened him to this type of labor, and he worked hard. Not only did it help him keep his mind off Allie during the day, but it was something he felt he had to do. His daddy had always said: "Give a day's work for a day's pay. Anything less is stealing." That attitude pleased his boss. "It's a shame you aren't Jewish," Goldman would say, "you're such a fine boy in so many other ways." It was the best compliment Goldman could give.

He continued to think about Allie, especially at night. He wrote her once a month but never received a reply. Eventually he wrote a final letter and forced himself to accept the fact that the summer they'd spent with one another was the only thing they'd ever share.

Still, though, she stayed with him. Three years after the last letter, he went to Winston-Salem in the hope of finding her. He went to her house, discovered that she had moved, and after talking to some neighbors, finally called RJR. The girl who answered the phone was new and didn't recognize the name, but she poked around the personnel files for him. She found out that Allie's father had left the company and that no forwarding address was listed. That trip was the first and last time he ever looked for her.

For the next eight years, he worked for Goldman. At first he was one of twelve employees, but as the years dragged on, the company grew, and he was promoted. By 1940 he had mastered the business and was running the entire operation, brokering the deals and managing a staff of thirty. The yard had become the largest scrap metal dealer on the East Coast.

During that time, he dated a few different women. He became serious with one, a waitress from the local diner with deep blue eyes and silky black hair. Although they dated for two years and had many good times together, he never came to feel the same way about her as he did about Allie.

But neither did he forget her. She was a few years older than he was, and it was she who taught him the ways to please a woman, the places to touch and kiss, where to linger, the things to whisper. They would sometimes spend an entire day in bed, holding each other and making the kind of love that fully satisfied both of them.

She had known they wouldn't be together forever. Toward the end of their relationship she'd told him once, "I wish I could give you what you're looking for, but I don't know what it is. There's a part of you that you keep closed off from everyone, including me. It's as if I'm not the one you're really with. Your mind is on someone else."

He tried to deny it, but she didn't believe him. "I'm a woman—I know these things. When you look at me sometimes, I know you're seeing someone else. It's like you keep waiting for her to pop out of thin air to take you away from all this. . . ." A month later she visited him at work and told him she'd met someone else. He understood. They parted as friends, and the following year he received a postcard from her saying she was married. He hadn't heard from her since.

While he was in New Jersey, he would visit his father once a year around Christmas. They'd spend some time fishing and talking, and once in a while they'd take a trip to the coast to go camping on the Outer Banks near Ocracoke.

In December 1941, when he was twenty-six, the war began, just as Goldman had predicted. Noah walked into his office the following month and informed Goldman of his intent to enlist, then returned to New Bern to say good-bye to his father. Five weeks later he found himself in boot camp. While there, he received a letter from Goldman thanking him for his work, together with a copy of a certificate entitling him to a small percentage of the scrap yard if it ever sold. "I couldn't have done it without you," the letter said. "You're the finest young man who ever worked for me, even if you aren't Jewish."

He spent his next three years with Patton's Third Army, tramping through deserts in North Africa and forests in Europe with thirty pounds on his back, his infantry unit never far from action. He watched his friends die around him; watched as some of them were buried thousands of miles from home. Once, while hiding in a fox-hole near the Rhine, he imagined he saw Allie watching over him.

He remembered the war ending in Europe, then a few months later in Japan. Just before he was discharged, he received a letter from a lawyer in New Jersey representing Morris Goldman. Upon meeting the lawyer, he found out that Goldman had died a year earlier and his estate liquidated. The business had been sold, and Noah was given a check for almost seventy thousand dollars. For some reason he was oddly unexcited about it.

The following week he returned to New Bern and bought the house. He remembered bringing his father around later, showing him what he was going to do, pointing out the changes he intended to make. His father seemed weak as he walked around, coughing and wheezing. Noah was concerned, but his father told him not to worry, assuring him that he had the flu.

Less than one month later his father died of pneumonia and was buried next to his wife in the local cemetery. Noah tried to stop by regularly to leave some flowers; occasionally he left a note. And every night without fail he took a moment to remember him, then said a prayer for the man who'd taught him everything that mattered.

After reeling in the line, he put the gear away and went back to the house. His neighbor, Martha Shaw, was there to thank him, bringing three loaves of homemade bread and some biscuits in appreciation for what he'd done. Her husband had been killed in the war, leaving her with three children and a tired shack of a house to raise them in. Winter was coming, and he'd spent a few days at her place last week repairing her roof, replacing broken windows and sealing the others, and fixing her woodstove. Hopefully, it would be enough to get them through.

Once she'd left, he got in his battered Dodge truck and went to see Gus. He always stopped there when he was going to the store because Gus's family didn't have a car. One of the daughters hopped up and rode with him, and they did their shopping at Capers General Store. When he got home he didn't unpack the groceries right away. Instead he showered, found a Budweiser and a book by Dylan Thomas, and went to sit on the porch.

She still had trouble believing it, even as she held the proof in her hands.

It had been in the newspaper at her parents'

house three Sundays ago. She had gone to the kitchen to get a cup of coffee, and when she'd returned to the table, her father had smiled and pointed at a small picture. "Remember this?"

He handed her the paper, and after an uninterested first glance, something in the picture caught her eye and she took a closer look. "It can't be," she whispered, and when her father looked at her curiously, she ignored him, sat down, and read the article without speaking. She vaguely remembered her mother coming to the table and sitting opposite her, and when she finally put aside the paper, her mother was staring at her with the same expression her father had just moments before.

"Are you okay?" her mother asked over her coffee cup. "You look a little pale." She didn't answer right away, she couldn't, and it was then that she'd noticed her hands were shaking. That had been when it started.

"And here it will end, one way or the other," she whispered again. She refolded the scrap of paper and put it back, remembering that she had left her parents' home later that day with the paper so she could cut out the article. She read it again before she went to bed that night, trying to fathom the coincidence, and read it again the next morning as if to make sure the whole thing wasn't a dream. And now, after three weeks of long walks alone, after three weeks of distraction, it was the reason she'd come.

When asked, she said her erratic behavior was due to stress. It was the perfect excuse; everyone understood, including Lon, and that's why he hadn't argued when she'd wanted to get away for a couple of days. The wedding plans were stressful to everyone involved. Almost five hundred people were invited, including the governor, one senator, and the ambassador to Peru. It was too much, in her opinion, but their engagement was news and had dominated the social pages since they had announced their plans six months ago. Occasionally she felt like running away with Lon to get married without the fuss. But she knew he wouldn't agree; like the aspiring politician he was, he loved being the center of attention.

She took a deep breath and stood again. "It's now or never," she whispered, then picked up her things and went to the door. She paused only slightly before opening it and going downstairs. The manager smiled as she walked by, and she could feel his eyes on her as she left and went to her car. She slipped behind the wheel, looked at herself one last time, then started the engine and turned right onto Front Street.

She wasn't surprised that she still knew her way around town so well. Even though she hadn't been here in years, it wasn't large and she navigated the streets easily. After crossing the Trent River on an old-fashioned drawbridge, she turned onto a gravel road and began the final leg of her journey.

It was beautiful here in the low country, as it always had been. Unlike the Piedmont area where she grew up, the land was flat, but it had the same silty, fertile soil that was ideal for cotton and tobacco. Those two crops and timber kept the towns alive in this part of the state, and as she drove along the road outside town, she saw the beauty that had first attracted people to this region.

To her, it hadn't changed at all. Broken sunlight passed through water oaks and hickory trees a hundred feet tall, illuminating the colors of fall. On her left, a river the color of iron veered toward the road and then turned away before giving up its life to a different, larger river another mile ahead. The gravel road itself wound its way between antebellum farms, and she knew that for some of the farmers, life hadn't changed since before their grandparents were born. The constancy of the place brought back a flood of memories, and she felt her insides tighten as one by one she recognized landmarks she'd long since forgotten.

The sun hung just above the trees on her left, and as she rounded a curve, she passed an old church, abandoned for years but still standing. She had explored it that summer, looking for souvenirs from the War between the States, and as her car passed by, the memories of that day became stronger, as if they'd just happened yesterday.

A majestic oak tree on the banks of the river came into view next, and the memories became more intense. It looked the same as it had back then, branches low and thick, stretching horizontally along the ground with Spanish moss draped over the limbs like a veil. She remembered sitting beneath the tree on a hot July day with someone who looked at her with a longing that took everything else away. And it had been at that moment that she'd first fallen in love.

He was two years older than she was, and as she drove along this roadway-in-time, he slowly came into focus once again. He always looked older than he really was, she remembered thinking. His appearance was that of someone slightly weathered, almost like a farmer coming home after hours in the field. He had the callused hands and broad shoulders that came to those who worked hard for a living, and the first faint lines were beginning to form around the dark eyes that seemed to read her every thought.

He was tall and strong, with light brown hair, and handsome in his own way, but it was his voice that she remembered most of all. He had read to her that day; read to her as they lay in the grass beneath the tree with an accent that was soft and fluent, almost musical in quality. It was the kind of voice that belonged on radio, and it seemed to hang in the air when he read to her. She remembered closing her eyes, listening closely, and letting the words he was reading touch her soul:

It coaxes me to the vapor and the dusk.

I depart as air, I shake my white locks at
the runaway sun . . .

He thumbed through old books with dog-
eared pages, books he'd read a hundred times.
He'd read for a while, then stop, and the two of
them would talk. She would tell him what she
wanted in her life—her hopes and dreams for the
future—and he would listen intently and then
promise to make it all come true. And the way he
said it made her believe him, and she knew then
how much he meant to her. Occasionally, when
she asked, he would talk about himself or
explain why he had chosen a particular poem
and what he thought of it, and at other times he
just studied her in that intense way of his.

They watched the sun go down and ate
together under the stars. It was getting late by
then, and she knew her parents would be furious
if they knew where she was. At that moment,
though, it really didn't matter to her. All she
could think about was how special the day had
been, how special he was, and as they started
toward her house a few minutes later, he took
her hand in his and she felt the way it warmed
her the whole way back.

Another turn in the road and she finally saw it
in the distance. The house had changed dramat-
ically from what she remembered. She slowed

the car as she approached, turning into the long, tree-lined dirt drive that led to the beacon that had summoned her from Raleigh.

She drove slowly, looking toward the house, and took a deep breath when she saw him on the porch, watching her car. He was dressed casually. From a distance, he looked the same as he had back then. For a moment, when the light from the sun was behind him, he almost seemed to vanish into the scenery.

Her car continued forward, rolling slowly, then finally stopped beneath an oak tree that shaded the front of the house. She turned the key, never taking her eyes from him, and the engine sputtered to a halt.

He stepped off the porch and began to approach her, walking easily, then suddenly stopped cold as she emerged from the car. For a long time all they could do was stare at each other without moving.

Allison Nelson, twenty-nine years old and engaged, a socialite, searching for answers she needed to know, and Noah Calhoun, the dreamer, thirty-one, visited by the ghost that had come to dominate his life.

Reunion

Neither one of them moved as they faced each other.

He hadn't said anything, his muscles seemed frozen, and for a second she thought he didn't recognize her. Suddenly she felt guilty about showing up this way, without warning, and this made it harder. She had thought it would be easier somehow, that she would know what to say. But she didn't. Everything that came into her head seemed inappropriate, somehow lacking.

Thoughts of the summer they'd shared came back to her, and as she stared at him, she noticed how little he'd changed since she'd last seen him. He looked good, she thought. With his shirt tucked loosely into old faded jeans, she could see the same broad shoulders she remembered, tapering down to narrow hips and a flat stomach. He was tan, too, as if he'd worked outside all summer, and though his hair was a little thinner and lighter than she remembered, he looked the same as he had when she'd known him last.

When she was finally ready, she took a deep breath and smiled.

"Hello, Noah. It's good to see you again."

Her comment startled him, and he looked at her with amazement in his eyes. Then, after shaking his head slightly, he slowly began to smile.

"You too . . . ," he stammered. He brought his hand to his chin, and she noticed he hadn't shaved. "It's really you, isn't it? I can't believe it. . . ."

She heard the shock in his voice as he spoke, and surprising her, it all came together—being here, seeing him. She felt something twitch inside, something deep and old, something that made her dizzy for just a second.

She caught herself fighting for control. She hadn't expected this to happen, didn't want it to happen. She was engaged now. She hadn't come here for this . . . yet . . .

Yet . . .

Yet the feeling went on despite herself, and for a brief moment she felt fifteen again. Felt as she hadn't in years, as if all her dreams could still come true.

Felt as though she'd finally come home.

Without another word they came together, as

if it were the most natural thing in the world, and he put his arms around her, drawing her close. They held each other tightly, making it real, both of them letting the fourteen years of separation dissolve in the deepening twilight.

They stayed like that for a long time before she finally pulled back to look at him. Up close, she could see the changes she hadn't noticed at first. He was a man now, and his face had lost the softness of youth. The faint lines around his eyes had deepened, and there was a scar on his chin that hadn't been there before. There was a new edge to him; he seemed less innocent, more cautious, and yet the way he was holding her made her realize how much she'd missed him since she'd seen him last.

Her eyes brimmed with tears as they finally released each other. She laughed nervously under her breath while wiping the tears from the corners of her eyes.

"Are you okay?" he asked, a thousand other questions on his face.

"I'm sorry, I didn't mean to cry. . . ."

"It's okay," he said, smiling, "I still can't believe it's you. How did you find me?"

She stepped back, trying to compose herself, wiping away the last of her tears.

"I saw the story on the house in the Raleigh paper a couple of weeks ago, and I had to come see you again."

Noah smiled broadly. "I'm glad you did." He

stepped back just a bit. "God, you look fantastic. You're even prettier now than you were then."

She felt the blood in her face. Just like fourteen years ago.

"Thank you. You look great, too." And he did, no doubt about it. The years had treated him well.

"So what have you been up to? Why are you here?"

His questions brought her back to the present, making her realize what could happen if she wasn't careful. Don't let this get out of hand, she told herself; the longer it goes on, the harder it's going to be. And she didn't want it to get any harder.

But God, those eyes. Those soft, dark eyes.

She turned away and took a deep breath, wondering how to say it, and when she finally started, her voice was quiet. "Noah, before you get the wrong idea, I did want to see you again, but there's more to it than just that." She paused for a second. "I came here for a reason. There's something I have to tell you."

"What is it?"

She looked away and didn't answer for a moment, surprised that she couldn't tell him just yet. In the silence, Noah felt a sinking feeling in his stomach. Whatever it was, was bad.

"I don't know how to say it. I thought I did at first, but now I'm not so sure. . . ."

The air was suddenly rattled by the sharp cry of a raccoon, and Clem came out from under the porch, barking gruffly. Both of them turned at the commotion, and Allie was glad for the distraction.

"Is he yours?" she asked.

Noah nodded, feeling the tightness in his stomach. "Actually it's a she. Clementine's her name. But yeah, she's all mine." They both watched as Clem shook her head, stretched, then wandered toward the sounds. Allie's eyes widened just a bit when she saw her limp away.

"What happened to her leg?" she asked, stalling for time.

"Hit by a car a few months back. Doc Harrison, the vet, called me to see if I wanted her because her owner didn't anymore. After I saw what had happened, I guess I just couldn't let her be put down."

"You were always nice like that," she said, trying to relax. She paused, then looked past him toward the house. "You did a wonderful job restoring it. It looks perfect, just like I knew it would someday."

He turned his head in the same direction as hers while he wondered about the small talk and what she was holding back.

"Thanks, that's nice of you. It was quite a project, though. I don't know if I would do it again."

"Of course you would," she said. She knew

exactly how he felt about this place. But then, she knew how he felt about everything—or at least she had a long time ago.

And with that thought, she realized how much had changed since then. They were strangers now; she could tell by looking at him. Could tell that fourteen years apart was a long time. Too long.

"What is it, Allie?" He turned to her, compelling her to look, but she continued to stare at the house.

"I'm being rather silly, aren't I?" she asked, trying to smile.

"What do you mean?"

"This whole thing. Showing up out of the blue, not knowing what I want to say. You must think I'm crazy."

"You're not crazy," he said gently. He reached for her hand, and she let him hold it as they stood next to one another. He went on:

"Even though I don't know why, I can see this is hard for you. Why don't we go for a walk?"

"Like we used to?"

"Why not? I think we both could use one."

She hesitated and looked to his front door. "Do you need to tell anyone?"

He shook his head.

"No, there's no one to tell. It's just me and Clem."

Even though she'd asked, she had suspected there wouldn't be anyone else, and inside she didn't know how to feel about that. But it did make what she wanted to say a little harder. It would have been easier if there was someone else.

They started toward the river and turned on a path near the bank. She let go of his hand, surprising him, and walked on with just enough distance between them so that they couldn't accidentally touch.

He looked at her. She was pretty still, with thick hair and soft eyes, and she moved so gracefully that it almost seemed as though she were gliding. He'd seen beautiful women before, though, women who caught his eye, but to his mind they usually lacked the traits he found most desirable. Traits like intelligence, confidence, strength of spirit, passion, traits that inspired others to greatness, traits he aspired to himself.

Allie had those traits, he knew, and as they walked now, he sensed them once again lingering beneath the surface. "A living poem" had always been the words that came to mind when he tried to describe her to others.

"How long have you been back here?" she asked as the path gave way to a small grass hill.

"Since last December. I worked up north for a while, then spent the last three years in Europe."

She looked to him with questions in her eyes. "The war?"

He nodded and she went on.

"I thought you might be there. I'm glad you made it out okay."

"Me too," he said.

"Are you glad to be back home?"

"Yeah. My roots are here. This is where I'm supposed to be." He paused. "But what about you?" He asked the question softly, suspecting the worst.

It was a long moment before she answered.

"I'm engaged."

He looked down when she said it, suddenly feeling just a bit weaker. So that was it. That's what she needed to tell him.

"Congratulations," he finally said, wondering how convincing he sounded. "When's the big day?"

"Three weeks from Saturday. Lon wanted a November wedding."

"Lon?"

"Lon Hammond Jr. My fiancé."

He nodded, not surprised. The Hammonds were one of the most powerful and influential families in the state. Cotton money. Unlike that of his own father, the death of Lon Hammond Sr. had made the front page of the newspaper. "I've heard of them. His father built quite a business. Did Lon take over for him?"

She shook her head. "No, he's a lawyer. He has his own practice downtown."

"With his name, he must be busy."

"He is. He works a lot."

He thought he heard something in her tone, and the next question came automatically.

"Does he treat you well?"

She didn't answer right away, as if she were considering the question for the first time. Then:

"Yes. He's a good man, Noah. You would like him."

Her voice was distant when she answered, or at least he thought it was. Noah wondered if it was just his mind playing tricks on him.

"How's your daddy doing?" she asked.

Noah took a couple of steps before answering. "He passed on earlier this year, right after I got back."

"I'm sorry," she said softly, knowing how much he had meant to Noah.

He nodded, and the two walked in silence for a moment.

They reached the top of the hill and stopped. The oak tree was in the distance, with the sun glowing orange behind it. Allie could feel his eyes on her as she stared in that direction.

"A lot of memories there, Allie."

She smiled. "I know. I saw it when I came in. Do you remember the day we spent there?"

"Yes," he answered, volunteering no more.

"Do you ever think about it?"

"Sometimes," he said. "Usually when I'm working out this way. It sits on my property now."

"You bought it?"

"I just couldn't bear to see it turned into kitchen cabinets."

She laughed under her breath, feeling strangely pleased about that. "Do you still read poetry?"

He nodded. "Yeah. I never stopped. I guess it's in my blood."

"Do you know, you're the only poet I've ever met."

"I'm no poet. I read, but I can't write a verse. I've tried."

"You're still a poet, Noah Taylor Calhoun." Her voice softened. "I still think about it a lot. It was the first time anyone ever read poetry to me before. In fact, it's the only time."

Her comment made both of them drift back and remember as they slowly circled back to the house, following a new path that passed near the dock. As the sun dropped a little lower and the sky turned orange, he asked:

"So, how long are you staying?"

"I don't know. Not long. Maybe until tomorrow or the next day."

"Is your fiancé here on business?"

She shook her head. "No, he's still in Raleigh."

Noah raised his eyebrows. "Does he know you're here?"

She shook her head again and answered slowly. "No. I told him I was looking for antiques. He wouldn't understand my coming here."

Noah was a little surprised by her answer. It was one thing to come and visit, but it was an entirely different matter to hide the truth from her fiancé.

"You didn't have to come here to tell me you were engaged. You could have written me instead, or even called."

"I know. But for some reason, I had to do it in person."

"Why?"

She hesitated. "I don't know . . . ," she said, trailing off, and the way she said it made him believe her. The gravel crunched beneath their feet as they walked in silence for a few steps. Then he asked:

"Allie, do you love him?"

She answered automatically. "Yes, I love him."

The words hurt. But again, he thought he heard something in her tone, as if she were saying it to convince herself. He stopped and gently took her shoulders in his hands, making her face him. The fading sunlight reflected in her eyes as he spoke.

"If you're happy, Allie, and you love him, I won't try to stop you from going back to him. But if there's a part of you that isn't sure, then don't do it. This isn't the kind of thing you go into halfway."

Her answer came almost too quickly.

"I'm making the right decision, Noah."

He stared for a second, wondering if he believed her. Then he nodded and the two began to walk again. After a moment he said: "I'm not making this easy for you, am I?"

She smiled a little. "It's okay. I really can't blame you."

"I'm sorry anyway."

"Don't be. There's no reason to be sorry. I'm the one who should be apologizing. Maybe I should have written."

He shook his head. "To be honest, I'm still glad you came. Despite everything. It's good to see you again."

"Thank you, Noah."

"Do you think it would be possible to start over?"

She looked at him curiously.

"You were the best friend I ever had, Allie. I'd still like to be friends, even if you are engaged, and even if it is just for a couple of days. How about we just kind of get to know each other again?"

She thought about it, thought about staying or leaving, and decided that since he knew about her engagement, it would probably be all right. Or at least not wrong. She smiled slightly and nodded.

"I'd like that."

"Good. How about dinner? I know a place that serves the best crab in town."

"Sounds great. Where?"

"My house. I've had the traps out all week, and I saw that I had some good ones caged a couple days ago. Do you mind?"

"No, that sounds fine."

He smiled and pointed over his shoulder with his thumb. "Great. They're at the dock. I'll just be a couple of minutes."

Allie watched him walk away and noticed the tension she'd felt when telling him about her engagement was beginning to fade. Closing her eyes, she ran her hands through her hair and let the light breeze fan her cheek. She took a deep breath and held it for a moment, feeling the muscles in her shoulders further relax as she exhaled. Finally, opening her eyes, she stared at the beauty that surrounded her.

She always loved evenings like this, evenings where the faint aroma of autumn leaves rode on the backs of soft southern winds. She loved the trees and the sounds they made. Listening to them helped her relax even more. After a moment, she turned toward Noah and looked at him almost as a stranger might.

God, he looked good. Even after all this time.

She watched him as he reached for a rope that hung in the water. He began to pull it, and despite the darkening sky, she saw the muscles in his arm flex as he lifted the cage from the water. He let it hang over the river for a moment and shook it, letting most of the water escape. After setting the trap on the dock, he opened it and began to remove the crabs one by one, placing them into a bucket.

She started walking toward him then, listening to the crickets chirp, and remembered a lesson from childhood. She counted the number of chirps in a minute and added twenty-nine. Sixty-seven degrees, she thought as she smiled to herself. She didn't know if it was accurate, but it felt about right.

As she walked, she looked around and realized she had forgotten how fresh and beautiful everything seemed here. Over her shoulder, she saw the house in the distance. He had left a couple of lights on, and it seemed to be the only house around. At least the only one with electricity. Out here, outside the town limits, nothing was certain. Thousands of country homes still lacked the luxury of indoor lighting.

She stepped on the dock and it creaked under her foot. The sound reminded her of a rusty squeeze-box, and Noah glanced up and winked, then went back to checking the crabs, making sure they were the right size. She walked to the rocker that sat on the dock and touched it, running her hand along the back. She could picture him sitting in it, fishing, thinking, reading. It was old and weather-beaten, rough feeling. She wondered how much time he spent here alone, and she wondered about his thoughts at times like those.

"It was my daddy's chair," he said, not looking up, and she nodded. She saw bats in the sky, and frogs had joined the crickets in their evening harmony.

She walked to the other side of the dock, feeling a sense of closure. A compulsion had driven her here, and for the first time in three weeks the feeling was gone. She'd somehow needed Noah to know about her engagement, to understand, to accept it—she was sure of that now—and while thinking of him, she was reminded of something they'd shared from the summer they were together. With head down, she paced around slowly, looking for it until she found it— the carving. *Noah loves Allie,* in a heart. Carved into the dock a few days before she'd left.

A breeze broke the stillness and chilled her, making her cross her arms. She stood that way, alternately looking down at the carving and then toward the river, until she heard him reach her side. She could feel his closeness, his warmth, as she spoke.

"It's so peaceful here," she said, her voice dreamlike.

"I know. I come down here a lot now just to be close to the water. It makes me feel good."

"I would, too, if I were you."

"Come on, let's go. The mosquitoes are getting vicious, and I'm starved."

The sky had turned black, and Noah started toward the house, Allie right beside him. In the silence her mind wandered, and she felt a little light-headed as she walked along the path. She wondered what he was thinking about her being here and wasn't exactly sure if she knew herself. When they reached the house a couple of minutes later, Clem greeted them with a wet nose in the wrong place. Noah motioned her away, and she left with her tail between her legs.

He pointed to her car. "Did you leave anything in there that you need to get out?"

"No, I got in earlier and unpacked already." Her voice sounded different to her, as if the years had suddenly been undone.

"Good enough," he said as he reached the back porch and started up the steps. He set the bucket by the door, then led the way inside, heading toward the kitchen. It was on the immediate right, large and smelling of new wood. The cabinets had been done in oak, as was the floor, and the windows were large and faced east, allowing the light from morning sun. It was a tasteful restoration, not overdone as was common when homes like this were rebuilt.

"Do you mind if I look around?"

"No, go ahead. I did some shopping earlier, and I still have to put the groceries away."

Their eyes met for a second, and Allie knew as she turned that he continued to watch her as she left the room. Inside she felt that little twitch again.

She toured the house for the next few minutes,

walking through the rooms, noticing how wonderful it looked. By the time she'd finished, it
was hard to remember how run-down it had
been. She came down the stairs, turned toward
the kitchen, and saw his profile. For a second he
looked like a young man of seventeen again, and
it made her pause a split second before going on.
Damn, she thought, get a hold of yourself.
Remember that you're engaged now.

He was standing by the counter, a couple of
cabinet doors open wide, empty grocery bags on
the floor, whistling quietly. He smiled at her
before putting a few more cans into one of the
cabinets. She stopped a few feet from him and
leaned against the counter, one leg over the other.
She shook her head, amazed at how much he had
done.

"It's unbelievable, Noah. How long did the
restoration take?"

He looked up from the last bag he was
unpacking. "Almost a year."

"Did you do it yourself?"

He laughed under his breath. "No. I always
thought I would when I was young, and I started that way. But it was just too much. It would
have taken years, and so I ended up hiring some
people . . . actually a lot of people. But even with
them, it was still a lot of work, and most of the
time I didn't stop until past midnight."

"Why'd you work so hard?"

Ghosts, he wanted to say, but didn't.

"I don't know. Just wanted to finish, I guess. Do you want anything to drink before I start dinner?"

"What do you have?"

"Not much, really. Beer, tea, coffee."

"Tea sounds good."

He gathered the grocery bags and put them away, then walked to a small room off the kitchen before returning with a box of tea. He pulled out a couple of teabags and set them by the stove, then filled the teapot. After putting it on the burner, he lit a match, and she heard the sound of flames as they came to life.

"It'll be just a minute," he said. "This stove heats up pretty quick."

"That's fine."

When the teapot whistled, he poured two cups and handed one to her.

She smiled and took a sip, then motioned toward the window. "I'll bet the kitchen is beautiful when the morning light shines in."

He nodded. "It is. I had larger windows put in on this side of the house for just that reason. Even in the bedrooms upstairs."

"I'm sure your guests enjoy that. Unless of course they want to sleep late."

"Actually, I haven't had any guests stay over yet. Since my daddy passed on, I don't really know who to invite."

By his tone, she knew he was just making conversation. Yet for some reason it made her feel . . . lonely. He seemed to realize how she was feeling, but before she could dwell on it, he changed the subject.

"I'm going to get the crabs in to marinate for a few minutes before I steam 'em," he said, putting his cup on the counter. He went to the cupboard and removed a large pot with a steamer and lid. He brought the pot to the sink, added water, then carried it to the stove.

"Can I give you a hand with something?"

He answered over his shoulder. "Sure. How about cutting up some vegetables for the fryer. There's plenty in the icebox, and you can find a bowl over there."

He motioned to the cabinet near the sink, and she took another sip of tea before setting her cup on the counter and retrieving the bowl. She carried it to the icebox and found some okra, zucchini, onions, and carrots on the bottom shelf. Noah joined her in front of the open door, and she moved to make room for him. She could smell him as he stood next to her—clean, familiar, distinctive—and felt his arm brush against her as he leaned over and reached inside. He removed a beer and a bottle of hot sauce, then returned to the stove.

Noah opened the beer and poured it in the water, then added the hot sauce and some other seasoning as well. After stirring the water to make sure the powders were dissolved, he went to the back door to get the crabs.

He paused for a moment before going back inside and stared at Allie, watching her cut the carrots. As he did that, he wondered again why she had come, especially now that she was engaged. None of this seemed to make much sense to him.

But then, Allie had always been surprising.

He smiled to himself, remembering back to the way she had been. Fiery, spontaneous, passionate—as he imagined most artists to be. And she was definitely that. Artistic talent like hers was a gift. He remembered seeing some paintings in the museums in New York and thinking that her work was just as good as what he had seen there.

She had given him a painting before she'd left that summer. It hung above the fireplace in the living room. She'd called it a picture of her dreams, and to him it had seemed extremely sensual. When he looked at it, and he often did late in the evening, he could see desire in the colors and the lines, and if he focused carefully, he could imagine what she had been thinking with every stroke.

A dog barked in the distance, and Noah realized he had been standing with the door open a long time. He quickly closed it, turning back to the kitchen. And as he walked, he wondered if she had noticed how long he'd been gone.

"How's it going?" he asked, seeing she was almost finished.

"Good. I'm almost done here. Anything else for dinner?"

"I have some homemade bread that I was planning on."

"Homemade?"

"From a neighbor," he said as he put the pail in the sink. He started the faucet and began to rinse the crabs, holding them under the water, then letting them scurry around the sink while he rinsed the next one. Allie picked up her cup and came over to watch him.

"Aren't you afraid they'll pinch you when you grab them?"

"No. Just grab 'em like this," he said, demonstrating, and she smiled.

"I forget you've done this your whole life."

"New Bern's small, but it does teach you how to do the things that matter."

She leaned against the counter, standing close to him, and emptied her cup. When the crabs were ready he put them in the pot on the stove. He washed his hands, turning to speak to her as he did so.

"You want to sit on the porch for a few minutes? I'd like to let 'em soak for a half hour."

"Sure," she said.

He wiped his hands, and together they went to the back porch. Noah flipped on the light as they went outside, and he sat in the older rocker, offering the newer one to her. When he saw her cup was empty, he went inside for a moment and emerged with another cup of tea and a beer for himself. He held out the cup and she took it, sipping again before she set it on the table beside the chairs.

"You were sitting out here when I came, weren't you?"

He answered as he made himself comfortable. "Yeah. I sit out here every night. It's a habit now."

"I can see why," she said as she looked around. "So, what is it you do these days?"

"Actually, I don't do anything but work on the house right now. It satisfies my creative urges."

"How can you . . . I mean . . ."

"Morris Goldman."

"Excuse me?"

He smiled. "My old boss from up north. His name was Morris Goldman. He offered me a part of the business just as I enlisted and died before I got home. When I got back to the States, his lawyers gave me a check big enough to buy this place and fix it up."

She laughed under her breath. "You always told me you'd find a way to do it."

They both sat quietly for a moment, thinking back again. Allie took another sip of tea.

"Do you remember sneaking over here the night you first told me about this place?"

He nodded, and she went on:

"I got home a little late that evening, and my parents were furious when I finally came in. I can still picture my daddy standing in the living room smoking a cigarette, my mother on the sofa staring straight ahead. I swear, they looked as if a family member had died. That was the first time my parents knew I was serious about you, and my mother had a long talk with me later that night. She said to me, 'I'm sure you think that I don't understand what you're going through, but I do. It's just that sometimes, our future is dictated by what we are, as opposed to what we want.' I remember being really hurt when she said that."

"You told me about it the next day. It hurt my feelings, too. I liked your parents, and I had no idea they didn't like me."

"It wasn't that they didn't like you. They didn't think you deserved me."

"There's not much difference."

There was a sadness in his voice when he responded, and she knew he was right to feel that way. She looked toward the stars while she ran her hand through her hair, pulling back the strands that had fallen onto her face.

"I know that. I always did. Maybe that's why my mother and I always seem to have a distance between us when we talk."

"How do you feel about it now?"

"The same as I did back then. That it's wrong,

that it isn't fair. It was a terrible thing for a girl to learn. That status is more important than feelings."

Noah smiled softly at her answer but said nothing.

"I've thought about you ever since that summer," she said.

"You have?"

"Why wouldn't you think so?" She seemed genuinely surprised.

"You never answered my letters."

"You wrote?"

"Dozens of letters. I wrote you for two years without receiving a single reply."

She slowly shook her head before lowering her eyes.

"I didn't know . . . ," she finally said, quietly, and he knew it must have been her mother, checking the mail, removing the letters without her knowledge. It was what he had always suspected, and he watched as Allie came to the same realization.

"It was wrong of her to do that, Noah, and I'm sorry she did. But try to understand. Once I left, she probably thought it would be easier for me to just let it go. She never understood how much you meant to me, and to be honest, I don't even know if she ever loved my father the way I loved you. In her mind, she was just trying to protect my feelings, and she probably thought the best way to do that was to hide the letters you sent."

"That wasn't her decision to make," he said quietly.

"I know."

"Would it have made a difference even if you'd got them?"

"Of course. I always wondered what you were up to."

"No, I mean with us. Do you think we would have made it?"

It took a moment for her to answer.

"I don't know, Noah. I really don't, and you don't either. We're not the same people we were then. We've changed, we've grown. Both of us."

She paused. He didn't respond, and in the silence she looked toward the creek. She went on:

"But yes, Noah, I think we would have. At least, I'd like to think we would have."

He nodded, looked down, then turned away.

"What's Lon like?"

She hesitated, not expecting the question. Bringing up Lon's name brought slight feelings of guilt to the surface, and for a moment she didn't know how to answer. She reached for her cup, took another sip of tea, and listened as a woodpecker tapped in the distance. She spoke quietly.

"Lon's handsome, charming, and successful, and most of my friends are insanely jealous. They think he's perfect, and in a lot of ways he is. He's kind to me, he makes me laugh, and I know he loves me in his own way." She paused for a moment, collecting her thoughts. "But there's always going to be something missing in our relationship."

She surprised herself with her answer but knew it was true nonetheless. And she also knew by looking at him that Noah had suspected the answer in advance.

"Why?"

She smiled weakly and shrugged as she answered. Her voice was barely above a whisper.

"I guess I still look for the kind of love we had that summer."

Noah thought about what she had said for a long while, thinking about the relationships he'd had since he'd last seen her.

"How about you?" she asked. "Did you ever think about us?"

"All the time. I still do."

"Are you seeing anyone?"

"No," he answered, shaking his head.

Both of them seemed to think about that, trying but finding it impossible to displace from their minds. Noah finished his beer, surprised that he had emptied it so quickly.

"I'm going to go start the water. Can I get you anything?"

She shook her head, and Noah went to the kitchen and put the crabs in the steamer and the bread in the oven. He found some flour and cornstarch for the vegetables, coated them, and put some grease into the frying pan. After turning the heat on low, he set a timer and pulled another beer from the icebox before heading back to the porch. And while he was doing those things, he thought about Allie and the love that was missing from both their lives.

Allie, too, was thinking. About Noah, about herself, about a lot of things. For a moment she wished she weren't engaged but then quickly cursed herself. It wasn't Noah she loved; she loved what they once had been. Besides, it was normal to feel this way. Her first real love, the only man she'd ever been with—how could she expect to forget him?

Yet was it normal for her insides to twitch whenever he came near? Was it normal to confess things she could never tell anyone else? Was it normal to come here three weeks from her wedding day?

"No, it's not," she finally whispered to herself as she looked to the evening sky. "There's nothing normal about any of this."

Noah came out at that moment and she smiled at him, glad he'd come back so she didn't have to think about it anymore. "It's going to take a few minutes," he said as he sat back down.

"That's fine. I'm not that hungry yet."

He looked at her then, and she saw the softness in his eyes. "I'm glad you came, Allie," he said.

"Me too. I almost didn't, though."

"Why did you come?"

I was compelled, she wanted to say, but didn't.

"Just to see you, to find out what you've been up to. To see how you are."

He wondered if that was all but didn't question further. Instead he changed the subject.

"By the way, I've been meaning to ask, do you still paint?"

She shook her head. "Not anymore."

He was stunned. "Why not? You have so much talent."

"I don't know. . . ."

"Sure you do. You stopped for a reason."

He was right. She'd had a reason.

"It's a long story."

"I've got all night," he answered.

"Did you really think I was talented?" she asked quietly.

"C'mon," he said, reaching for her hand, "I want to show you something."

She got up and followed him through the door to the living room. He stopped in front of the fireplace and pointed to the painting that hung above the mantel. She gasped, surprised she hadn't noticed it earlier, more surprised it was here at all.

"You kept it?"

"Of course I kept it. It's wonderful."

She gave him a skeptical look, and he explained.

"It makes me feel alive when I look at it. Sometimes I have to get up and touch it. It's just so real—the shapes, the shadows, the colors. I even dream about it sometimes. It's incredible, Allie—I can stare at it for hours."

"You're serious," she said, shocked.

"As serious as I've ever been."

She didn't say anything.

"You mean to tell me no one has ever told you that before?"

"My professor did," she finally said, "but I guess I didn't believe him."

He knew there was more. Allie looked away before continuing.

"I've been drawing and painting since I was a child. I guess that once I got a little older, I began to think I was good at it. I enjoyed it, too. I remember working on this painting that summer, adding to it every day, changing it as our relationship changed. I don't even remember how it started or what I wanted it to be, but somehow it evolved into this.

"I remember being unable to stop painting after I went home that summer. I think it was my way of avoiding the pain I was going through. Anyway, I ended up majoring in art in college because it was something I had to do; I remember spending hours in the studio all by myself and enjoying every minute. I loved the freedom I felt when I created, the way it made me feel inside to make something beautiful. Just before I graduated, my professor, who happened to also be the critic for the paper, told me I had a lot of talent. He told me I should try my luck as an artist. But I didn't listen to him."

She stopped there, gathering her thoughts.

"My parents didn't think it was proper for someone like me to paint for a living. I just stopped after a while. I haven't touched a brush in years."

She stared at the painting.

"Do you think you'll ever paint again?"

"I'm not sure if I can anymore. It's been a long time."

"You can still do it, Allie. I know you can. You have a talent that comes from inside you, from your heart, not from your fingers. What you have can't ever go away. It's what other people only dream about. You're an artist, Allie."

The words were spoken with such sincerity that she knew he wasn't saying it just to be nice. He truly believed in her ability, and for some reason that meant more to her than she expected. But something else happened then, something even more powerful.

Why it happened, she never knew, but this was when the chasm began to close for Allie, the chasm she had erected in her life to separate the pain from the pleasure. And she suspected then, maybe not consciously, that there was more to this than even she cared to admit.

But at that moment she still wasn't completely aware of it, and she turned to face him. She reached over and touched his hand, hesitantly, gently, amazed that after all these years he'd somehow known exactly what she'd needed to hear. When their eyes locked, she once again realized how special he was.

And for just a fleeting moment, a tiny wisp of time that hung in the air like fireflies in summer skies, she wondered if she was in love with him again.

The timer went off in the kitchen, a small *ding,* and Noah turned away, breaking the moment, strangely affected by what had just happened between them. Her eyes had spoken to him and whispered something he longed to hear, yet he couldn't stop the voice inside his head, her voice, that had told him of her love for another man. He silently cursed the timer as he walked to the kitchen and removed the bread from the oven. He almost burned his fingers, dropped the loaf on the counter, and saw that the frying pan was ready. He added the vegetables and heard them begin to crackle. Then, muttering to himself, he got some butter out of the icebox, spread some on the bread, and melted a bit more for the crabs.

Allie had followed him into the kitchen and cleared her throat.

"Can I get the table ready?"

Noah used the bread knife as a pointer. "Sure,

plates are over there. Utensils and napkins there. Make sure you get plenty—crabs can be messy, so we'll need 'em." He couldn't look at her as he spoke. He didn't want to realize he'd been mistaken about what had just happened between them. He didn't want it to be a mistake.

Allie, too, was wondering about the moment and feeling warm as she thought of it. The words he'd spoken replayed in her head as she found everything she needed for the table: plates, place settings, salt and pepper. Noah handed her the bread as she was finishing the table, and their fingers touched briefly.

He turned his attention back to the frying pan and turned the vegetables. He lifted the lid of the steamer, saw the crabs still had a minute, and let them cook some more. He was more composed now and returned to small talk, easy conversation.

"Have you ever had crab before?"

"A couple of times. But only in salads."

He laughed. "Then you're in for an adventure. Hold on a second." He disappeared upstairs for a moment, then returned with a navy blue button-down shirt. He held it open for her.

"Here, put this on. I don't want you to stain your dress."

Allie put it on and smelled the fragrance that lingered in the shirt—his smell, distinctive, natural.

"Don't worry," he said, seeing her expression, "it's clean."

She laughed. "I know. It just reminds me of our first real date. You gave me your jacket that night, remember?"

He nodded. "Yeah, I remember. Fin and Sarah were with us. Fin kept elbowing me the whole way back to your parents' house, trying to get me to hold your hand."

"You didn't, though."

"No," he answered, shaking his head.

"Why not?"

"Shy, maybe, or afraid. I don't know. It just didn't seem like the right thing to do at the time."

"Come to think of it, you were kind of shy, weren't you."

"I prefer the words 'quiet confidence,'" he answered with a wink, and she smiled.

The vegetables and crabs were ready about the same time. "Be careful, they're hot," he said as he handed them to her, and they sat across from each other at the small wooden table. Then, realizing the tea was still on the counter, Allie stood and brought it over. After putting some vegetables and bread on their plates, Noah added a crab, and Allie sat for a moment, staring at it.

"It looks like a bug."

"A good bug, though," he said. "Here, let me show you how it's done."

He demonstrated quickly, making it look easy, removing the meat and putting it on her plate.

Allie crushed the legs too hard the first time and the time after that, and had to use her fingers to get the shells away from the meat. She felt clumsy at first, worrying that he saw every mistake, but then she realized her own insecurity. He didn't care about things like that. He never had.

"So, whatever happened to Fin?" she asked.

It took a second for him to answer.

"Fin died in the war. His destroyer was torpedoed in forty-three."

"I'm sorry," she said. "I know he was a good friend of yours."

His voice changed, a little deeper now.

"He was. I think of him a lot these days. I especially remember the last time I saw him. I'd come home to say good-bye before I enlisted, and we ran into each other again. He was a banker here, like his daddy was, and he and I spent a lot of time together over the next week. Sometimes I think I talked him into joining. I don't think he would have, except that I was going to."

"That's not fair," she said, sorry she'd brought up the subject.

"You're right. I just miss him, is all."

"I liked him, too. He made me laugh."

"He was always good at that."

She looked at him slyly. "He had a crush on me, you know."

"I know. He told me about it."

"He did? What did he say?"

Noah shrugged. "The usual for him. That he had to fight you off with a stick. That you chased him constantly, that sort of thing."

She laughed quietly. "Did you believe him?"

"Of course," he answered, "why wouldn't I?"

"You men always stick together," she said as she reached across the table, poking his arm with her finger. She went on. "So, tell me everything you've been up to since I saw you last."

They started to talk then, making up for lost time. Noah talked about leaving New Bern, about working in the shipyard and at the scrap yard in New Jersey. He spoke fondly of Morris Goldman and touched on the war a little, avoiding most of the details, and told her about his father and how much he missed him. Allie talked about going to college, painting, and her hours spent volunteering at the hospital. She talked about her family and friends and the charities she was involved with. Neither of them brought up anybody they had dated since they'd last seen each other. Even Lon was ignored, and though both of them noticed the omission, neither mentioned it.

Afterward Allie tried to remember the last time she and Lon had talked this way. Although he listened well and they seldom argued, he was not the type of man to talk like this. Like her father, he wasn't comfortable sharing his thoughts and feelings. She'd tried to explain that she needed to be closer to him, but it had never seemed to make a difference.

But sitting here now, she realized what she'd been missing.

The sky grew darker and the moon rose higher as the evening wore on. And without either of them being conscious of it, they began to regain the intimacy, the bond of familiarity, they had once shared.

They finished dinner, both pleased with the meal, neither talking much now. Noah looked at his watch and saw that it was getting late. The stars were out in full, the crickets a little quieter. He had enjoyed talking to Allie and wondered if he'd talked too much, wondered what she'd thought about his life, hoping it would somehow make a difference, if it could.

Noah got up and refilled the teapot. They both brought the dishes to the sink and cleaned up the table, and he poured two more cups of hot water, adding teabags to both.

"How about the porch again?" he asked, handing her the cup, and she agreed, leading the way. He grabbed a quilt for her in case she got cold, and soon they had taken their places again, the quilt over her legs, rockers moving. Noah watched her from the corner of his eye. God, she's beautiful, he thought. And inside, he ached.

For something had happened during dinner.

Quite simply, he had fallen in love again. He knew that now as they sat next to one another.

Fallen in love with a new Allie, not just her memory.

But then, he had never really stopped, and this, he realized, was his destiny.

"It's been quite a night," he said, his voice softer now.

"Yes, it has," she said, "a wonderful night."

Noah turned to the stars, their twinkling lights reminding him that she would be leaving soon, and he felt almost empty inside. This was a night he wanted never to end. How should he tell her? What could he say that would make her stay?

He didn't know. And thus the decision was made to say nothing. And he realized then that he had failed.

The rockers moved in quiet rhythm. Bats again, over the river. Moths kissing the porch light. Somewhere, he knew, there were people making love.

"Talk to me," she finally said, her voice sensual. Or was his mind playing tricks?

"What should I say?"

"Talk like you did to me under the oak tree."

And he did, reciting distant passages, toasting the night. Whitman and Thomas, because he loved the images. Tennyson and Browning, because their themes felt so familiar.

She rested her head against the back of the rocker, closing her eyes, growing just a bit warmer by the time he'd finished. It wasn't just the poems or his voice that did it. It was all of it, the whole greater than the sum of the parts. She didn't try to break it down, didn't want to, because it wasn't meant to be listened to that way. Poetry, she thought, wasn't written to be analyzed; it was meant to inspire without reason, to touch without understanding.

Because of him, she'd gone to a few poetry readings offered by the English department while in college. She'd sat and listened to different people, different poems, but had stopped soon after, discouraged that no one inspired her or seemed as inspired as true lovers of poetry should be.

They rocked for a while, drinking tea, sitting quietly, drifting in their thoughts. The compulsion that had driven her here was gone now—she was glad for this—but she worried about the feelings that had taken its place, the stirrings that had begun to sift and swirl in her pores like gold dust in river pans. She'd tried to deny them, hide from them, but now she realized that she didn't want them to stop. It had been years since she'd felt this way.

Lon could not evoke these feelings in her. He never had and probably never would. Maybe that was why she had never been to bed with him. He had tried before, many times, using everything from flowers to guilt, and she had always used the excuse that she wanted to wait until marriage. He took it well, usually, and she sometimes wondered how hurt he would be if he ever found out about Noah.

But there was something else that made her want to wait, and it had to do with Lon himself. He was driven in his work, and it always commanded most of his attention. Work came first, and for him there was no time for poems and wasted evenings and rocking on porches. She knew this was why he was successful, and part of her respected him for that. But she also sensed it wasn't enough. She wanted something else, something different, something more. Passion and romance, perhaps, or maybe quiet conversations in candlelit rooms, or perhaps something as simple as not being second.

Noah, too, was sifting through his thoughts. To him, the evening would be remembered as one of the most special times he had ever had. As he rocked, he remembered it all in detail, then remembered it again. Everything she had done seemed somehow electric to him, charged.

Now, sitting beside her, he wondered if she'd ever dreamed the same things he had in the years they'd been apart. Had she ever dreamed of them holding each other again and kissing in soft moonlight? Or did she go further and dream of their naked bodies, which had been kept separate for far too long. . . .

He looked to the stars and remembered the thousands of empty nights he had spent since they'd last seen each other. Seeing her again brought all those feelings to the surface, and he found it impossible to press them back down. He knew then he wanted to make love to her again and to have her love in return. It was what he needed most in the world.

But he also realized it could never be. Now that she was engaged.

Allie knew by his silence that he was thinking about her and found that she reveled in it. She didn't know what his thoughts were exactly, didn't care really, just knew they were about her and that was enough.

She thought about their conversation at dinner and wondered about loneliness. For some reason she couldn't picture him reading poetry to someone else or even sharing his dreams with another woman. He didn't seem the type. Either that, or she didn't want to believe it.

She put down the tea, then ran her hands through her hair, closing her eyes as she did so.

"Are you tired?" he asked, finally breaking free from his thoughts.

"A little. I should really be going in a couple of minutes."

"I know," he said, nodding, his tone neutral.

She didn't get up right away. Instead she picked up the cup and drank the last swallow of tea, feeling it warm her throat. She took the evening in. Moon higher now, wind in the trees, temperature dropping.

She looked at Noah next. The scar on his face

was visible from the side. She wondered if it had happened during the war, then wondered if he'd ever been wounded at all. He hadn't mentioned it and she hadn't asked, mostly because she didn't want to imagine him being hurt.

"I should go," she finally said, handing the quilt back to him.

Noah nodded, then stood without a word. He carried the quilt, and the two of them walked to her car while fallen leaves crunched beneath their feet. She started to take off the shirt he'd loaned her as he opened the door, but he stopped her.

"Keep it," he said. "I want you to have it."

She didn't ask why, because she wanted to keep it, too. She readjusted it and crossed her arms afterward to ward off the chill. For some reason, as she stood there she was reminded of standing on her front porch after a high school dance, waiting for a kiss.

"I had a great time tonight," he said. "Thank you for finding me."

"I did, too," she answered.

He summoned his courage. "Will I see you tomorrow?"

A simple question. She knew what the answer should be, especially if she wanted to keep her life simple. "I don't think we should," was all she had to say, and it would end right here and now. But for a second she didn't say anything.

The demon of choice confronted her then,

teased her, challenged her. Why couldn't she say it? She didn't know. But as she looked in his eyes to find the answer she needed, she saw the man she'd once fallen in love with, and suddenly it all came clear.

"I'd like that."

Noah was surprised. He hadn't expected her to answer this way. He wanted to touch her then, to take her in his arms, but he didn't.

"Can you be here about noon?"

"Sure. What do you want to do?"

"You'll see," he answered. "I know just the place to go."

"Have I ever been there before?"

"No, but it's a special place."

"Where is it?"

"It's a surprise."

"Will I like it?"

"You'll love it," he said.

She turned away before he could attempt a kiss. She didn't know if he would try but knew for some reason that if he did, she would have a hard time stopping him. She couldn't handle that right now, with everything going through her head. She slid behind the wheel, breathing a sigh of relief. He shut the door for her, and she started the engine. As the car idled, she rolled down the window just a bit.

"See you tomorrow," she said, her eyes reflecting the moonlight.

Noah waved as she backed the car out. She

turned it around, then drove up the lane, heading toward town. He watched the car until the lights vanished behind far-off oak trees and the engine noise was gone. Clem wandered up to him and he squatted down to pet her, paying special attention to her neck, scratching the spot she couldn't reach anymore. After he looked up the road one last time, they returned to the back porch side by side.

He sat in the rocker again, this time alone, trying once again to fathom the evening that had just passed. Thinking about it. Replaying it. Seeing it again. Hearing it again. Running it by in slow motion. He didn't feel like playing his guitar now, didn't feel like reading. Didn't know what he felt.

"She's engaged," he finally whispered, and then was silent for hours, his rocker making the only noise. The night was quiet now, with little activity except for Clem, who visited him occasionally, checking on him as if to ask "Are you all right?"

And sometime after midnight on that clear October evening, it all rushed inward and Noah was overcome with longing. And if anyone had seen him, they would have seen what looked like an old man, someone who'd aged a lifetime in just a couple of hours. Someone bent over in his rocker with his face in his hands and tears in his eyes.

He didn't know how to stop them.

$\mathscr{P}$hone $\mathscr{C}$alls

$\mathbf{L}$on hung up the phone.

He had called at seven, then at eight-thirty, and now he checked his watch again. Nine forty-five.

Where was she?

He knew she was where she had said she would be because he had spoken to the manager earlier. Yes, she had checked in and he had last seen her around six. Going to dinner, he thought. No, he hadn't seen her since.

Lon shook his head and leaned back in his chair. He was the last one in the office, as usual, and everything was quiet. But that was normal with an ongoing trial, even if the trial was going well. Law was his passion, and the late hours alone gave him the opportunity to catch up on his work without interruption.

He knew he would win the case because he mastered the law and charmed the jury. He always did, and losses were infrequent now. Part of it came from being able to select the cases he had the expertise to win. He had reached that level in his practice. Only a select few in the city had that kind of stature, and his earnings reflected that.

But the more important part of his success came from hard work. He had always paid attention to details, especially when he'd begun his practice. Little things, obscure things, and it had become a habit now. Whether it was a matter of law or presentation, he was diligent in his study, and it had won him a few cases early in his career when he should have lost.

And now, a little detail bothered him.

Not about the case. No, that was fine. It was something else.

Something about Allie.

But damn, he couldn't put his finger on it. He was fine when she'd left this morning. At least he thought he was. But sometime after her call, maybe an hour or so, something clicked in his mind. The little detail.

Detail.

Something insignificant? Something important?

Think . . . think . . . Damn, what was it?

His mind clicked.

Something . . . something . . . *something said?*

Something had been said? Yes, that was it. He knew it. But what was it? Had Allie said anything on the phone? That had been when it started, and he ran through the conversation again. No, nothing out of the ordinary.

But that was it, he was sure now.

What had she said?

Her trip was good, she had checked in, had done some shopping. Left her number. That's about all.

He thought about her then. He loved her, he was sure of that. Not only was she beautiful and charming, but she'd become his source of stability and best friend as well. After a hard day at work, she was the first person he would call. She would listen to him, laugh at the right moments, and had a sixth sense about what he needed to hear.

But more than that, he admired the way she'd always spoken her mind. He remembered that after they'd gone out a few times, he'd said to her what he said to all women he dated—that he wasn't ready for a steady relationship. Unlike the others, though, Allie had simply nodded and said, "Fine." But on her way out the door, she'd turned and said: "But your problem isn't me, or your job, or your freedom, or whatever else you think it is. Your problem is that you're alone. Your father made the Hammond name famous, and you've probably been compared to him all your life. You've never been your own person. A life like that makes you empty inside, and you're looking for someone who will magically fill that void. But no one can do that but you."

The words had stayed with him that night and rung true the following morning. He'd called again, asked for a second chance, and after some persistence, she'd reluctantly agreed.

In the four years they'd dated, she'd become everything he ever wanted, and he knew he should spend more time with her. But practicing law made limiting his hours impossible. She'd always understood, but still, he cursed himself for not making the time. Once he was married, he'd shorten his hours, he promised himself. He'd have his secretary check his schedule to make sure he wasn't overextending himself. . . .

Check? . . .

And his mind clicked another notch.

Check . . . checking . . . *checking in?*

He looked to the ceiling. Checking in?

Yes, that was it. He closed his eyes and thought for a second. No. Nothing. What, then?

C'mon, don't fail now. Think, damn it, think.

New Bern.

The thought popped into his head just then. Yes, New Bern. That was it. The little detail, or part of it. What else, though?

New Bern, he thought again, and knew the name. Knew the town a little, mainly from a few trials he had been in. Stopped there a few times on the way to the coast. Nothing special. He and Allie had never been there together.

But Allie had been there before. . . .

And the rack tightened its grip, another part coming together.

Another part. . . but there was more. . . .

Allie, New Bern . . . and . . . and . . . something at a party. A comment in passing. From Allie's mother. He'd hardly noticed it. But what had she said?

And Lon paled then, remembering. Remembering what had been said so long ago. Remembering what Allie's mother had said.

It was something about Allie being in love one time with a young man from New Bern. Called it puppy love. So what, he had thought when he'd heard it, and had turned to smile at Allie.

But she hadn't smiled. She was angry. And then Lon guessed that she had loved that person far more deeply than her mother had suggested. Maybe even more deeply than she loved him.

And now she was there. Interesting.

Lon brought his palms together, as though he were praying, resting them against his lips. Coincidence? Could be nothing. Could be exactly what she said. Could be stress and antique shopping. Possible. Even probable.

Yet . . . yet . . . what if?

Lon considered the other possibility, and for the first time in a long time, he became frightened.

What if? *What if she's with him?*

He cursed the trial, wishing it were over. Wishing he had gone with her. Wondering if she'd told him the truth, hoping that she had.

And he made up his mind then not to lose her. He would do anything it took to keep her. She was everything he'd always needed, and he'd never find another quite like her.

So, with trembling hands, he dialed the phone for the fourth and last time that evening.

And again there was no answer.

Kayaks and
Forgotten Dreams

Allie woke early the next morning, forced by the incessant chirping of starlings, and rubbed her eyes, feeling the stiffness in her body. She hadn't slept well, waking after every dream, and she remembered seeing the hands of the clock in different positions during the night, as if verifying the passage of time.

She'd slept in the soft shirt he'd given her, and she smelled him once again while thinking about the evening they'd spent together. The easy laughter and conversation came back to her, and she especially remembered the way he'd talked about her painting. It was so unexpected, yet uplifting, and as the words began to replay in her mind, she realized how sorry she would have been had she decided not to see him again.

She looked out the window and watched the chattering birds search for food in early light. Noah, she knew, had always been a morning person who greeted dawn in his own way. She knew he liked to kayak or canoe, and she remembered the one morning she'd spent with him in his canoe, watching the sun come up. She'd had to sneak out her window to do it because her parents wouldn't allow it, but she hadn't been caught and she remembered how Noah had slipped his arm around her and pulled her close as dawn began to unfold. "Look there," he'd whispered, and she'd watched her first sunrise with her head on his shoulder, wondering if anything could be better than what was happening at that moment.

And as she got out of bed to take her bath, feeling the cold floor beneath her feet, she wondered if he'd been on the water this morning watching another day begin, thinking somehow he probably had.

She was right.

Noah was up before the sun and dressed quickly, same jeans as last night, undershirt, clean flannel shirt, blue jacket, and boots. He brushed his teeth before going downstairs, drank a quick glass of milk, and grabbed two biscuits on the way out the door. After Clem greeted him with a couple of sloppy licks, he walked to the dock where his kayak was stored. He liked to let the river work its magic, loosening up his muscles, warming his body, clearing his mind.

The old kayak, well used and river stained, hung on two rusty hooks attached to his dock just above the waterline to keep off the barnacles. He lifted it free from the hooks and set it at his feet, inspected it quickly, then took it to the bank. In a couple of seasoned moves long since mastered by habit, he had it in the water working its way upstream with himself as the pilot and engine.

The air was cool on his skin, almost crisp, and the sky was a haze of different colors: black directly above him like a mountain peak, then blues of infinite range, becoming lighter until it met the horizon, where gray took its place. He took a few deep breaths, smelling pine trees and brackish water, and began to reflect. This had been part of what he'd missed most when he had lived up north. Because of the long hours at work, there had been little time to spend on the water. Camping, hiking, paddling on rivers, dating, working . . . something had had to go. For the most part he'd been able to explore New Jersey's countryside on foot whenever he'd had extra time, but in fourteen years he hadn't canoed or kayaked once. It had been one of the first things he'd done when he returned.

There's something special, almost mystical, about spending dawn on the water, he thought to himself, and he did it almost every day now.

Sunny and clear or cold and bitter, it never mattered as he paddled in rhythm to music in his head, working above water the color of iron. He saw a family of turtles resting on a partially submerged log and watched as a heron broke for flight, skimming just above the water before vanishing into the silver twilight that preceded sunrise.

He paddled out to the middle of the creek, where he watched the orange glow begin to stretch across the water. He stopped paddling hard, giving just enough effort to keep him in place, staring until light began to break through the trees. He always liked to pause at daybreak—there was a moment when the view was spectacular, as if the world were being born again. Afterward he began to paddle hard, working off the tension, preparing for the day.

While he did that, questions danced in his mind like water drops in a frying pan. He wondered about Lon and what type of man he was, wondered about their relationship. Most of all, though, he wondered about Allie and why she had come.

By the time he reached home, he felt renewed. Checking his watch, he was surprised to find that it had taken two hours. Time always played tricks out there, though, and he'd stopped questioning it months ago.

He hung the kayak to dry, stretched for a couple of minutes, and went to the shed where he stored his canoe. He carried it to the bank, leaving it a few feet from the water, and as he turned toward the house, he noted that his legs were still a little stiff.

The morning haze hadn't burned off yet, and he knew the stiffness in his legs usually predicted rain. He looked to the western sky and saw storm clouds, thick and heavy, far off but definitely present. The winds weren't blowing hard, but they were bringing the clouds closer. From the looks of them, he didn't want to be outside when they got here. Damn. How much time did he have? A few hours, maybe more. Maybe less.

He showered, put on new jeans, a red shirt, and black cowboy boots, brushed his hair, and went downstairs to the kitchen. He did the dishes from the night before, picked up a little around the house, made himself some coffee, and went to the porch. The sky was darker now, and he checked the barometer. Steady, but it would start dropping soon. The western sky promised that.

He'd learned long ago to never underestimate the weather, and he wondered if it was a good idea to go out. The rain he could deal with; lightning was a different story. Especially if he was on the water. A canoe was no place to be when electricity sparked in humid air.

He finished his coffee, putting off the decision until later. He went to the toolshed and found his ax. After checking the blade by pressing his thumb to it, he sharpened it with a whetstone until it was ready. "A dull ax is more dangerous than a sharp one," his daddy used to say.

He spent the next twenty minutes splitting and stacking logs. He did it easily, his strokes efficient, and didn't break a sweat. He set a few logs off to the side for later and brought them inside when he was finished, putting them by the fireplace.

He looked at Allie's painting again and reached out to touch it, bringing back the feelings of disbelief at seeing her again. God, what was it about her that made him feel this way? Even after all these years? What sort of power did she have over him?

He finally turned away, shaking his head, and went back to the porch. He checked the barometer again. It hadn't changed. Then he looked at his watch.

Allie should be here soon.

Allie had finished her bath and was already dressed. Earlier she'd opened the window to check the temperature. It wasn't cold outside, and she'd decided on a cream-colored spring dress with long sleeves and a high neck. It was soft and comfortable, maybe a little snug, but it looked good, and she had selected some white sandals that matched.

She spent the morning walking around downtown. The Depression had taken its toll here, but she could see the signs of prosperity beginning to work their way back. The Masonic theater, the oldest active theater in the country, looked a little more run-down but was still operating with a couple of recent movies. Fort Totten Park looked exactly the same as it had fourteen years ago, and she assumed the kids who played on the swings after school looked the same as well. She smiled at the memory then, thinking back to when things were simpler. Or at least had seemed to be.

Now, it seemed, nothing was simple. It seemed so improbable, everything falling into place as it had, and she wondered what she would have been doing now, had she never seen the article in the paper. It wasn't very difficult to imagine, because her routines seldom changed. It was Wednesday, which meant bridge at the country club, then on to the Junior Women's League, where they would probably be arranging another fund-raiser for the private school or hospital. After that, a visit with her mother, then home to get ready for dinner with Lon, because he made it a point to leave work by seven. It was the one night a week she saw him regularly.

She suppressed a feeling of sadness about that, hoping that one day he would change. He had often promised to and usually followed through for a few weeks before drifting back to the same schedule. "I can't tonight, honey," he would always explain. "I'm sorry, but I can't. Let me make it up to you later."

She didn't like to argue with him about it, mostly because she knew he was telling the truth. Trial work was demanding, both beforehand and during, yet she couldn't help wondering sometimes why he had spent so much time courting her if he didn't want to spend the time with her now.

She passed an art gallery, almost walked by it in her preoccupation, then turned and went back. She paused at the door for a second, surprised at how long it had been since she'd been in one. At least three years, maybe longer. Why had she avoided it?

She went inside—it had opened with the rest of the shops on Front Street—and browsed among the paintings. Many of the artists were local, and there was a strong sea flavor to their works. Lots of ocean scenes, sandy beaches, pelicans, old sailing ships, tugboats, piers, and seagulls. But most of all, waves. Waves of every shape, size, and color imaginable, and after a while they all looked alike. The artists were either uninspired or lazy, she thought.

On one wall though, there were a few paintings that more suited her tastes. All were by an artist she'd never heard of, Elayn, and most appeared to have been inspired by the architecture of the Greek islands. In the painting she liked the best, she noted the artist had purposely

exaggerated the scene with smaller-than-life fig-
ures, wide lines, and heavy sweeps of color, as if
not completely focused. Yet the colors were vivid
and swirling, drawing the eye in, almost direct-
ing what it should see next. It was dynamic, dra-
matic. The more she thought about it, the more
she liked it, and she considered buying it before
she realized that she liked it because it reminded
her of her own work. She examined it more
closely and thought to herself that maybe Noah
was right. Maybe she should start painting
again.

At nine-thirty Allie left the gallery and went to
Hoffman-Lane, a department store downtown.
It took a few minutes to find what she was looking for, but it was there, in the school supply sec-
tion. Paper, drawing chalk, and pencils, not high
quality but good enough. It wasn't painting, but
it was a start, and she was excited by the time
she got back to her room. She sat at the desk and
started working: nothing specific, just getting the
feel of it again, letting shapes and colors flow
from the memory of her youth. After a few minutes of abstraction, she did a rough sketch of the
street scene as seen from her room, amazed at
how easily it came. It was almost as if she'd
never stopped.

She examined it when she was finished,
pleased with the effort. She wondered what to
try next and finally decided. Since she didn't
have a model, she visualized it in her head before

starting. And though it was harder than the street scene, it came naturally and began to take form.

Minutes passed quickly. She worked steadily but checked the time frequently so she wouldn't be late, and she finished it a little before noon. It had taken almost two hours, but the end result surprised her. It looked as though it had taken a great deal longer. After rolling it up, she put it in a bag and collected the rest of her things. On her way out the door, she looked at herself in the mirror, feeling oddly relaxed, not exactly sure why.

Down the stairs again and out the door. As she left she heard a voice behind her.

"Miss?"

She turned, knowing it was directed at her. The manager. Same man as yesterday, a curious look on his face.

"Yes?"

"You had some calls last night."

She was shocked. "I did?"

"Yes. All from a Mr. Hammond."

Oh, God.

"Lon called?"

"Yes, ma'am, four times. I talked to him when he called the second time. He was rather concerned about you. He said he was your fiancé."

She smiled weakly, trying to hide what she was thinking. Four times? Four? What could that mean? What if something had happened back home?

"Did he say anything? Is it an emergency?"

He shook his head quickly. "He really didn't say, miss, but he didn't mention anything. Actually, he sounded more concerned about you, though."

Good, she thought. That's good. And then, just as suddenly, a pang in her chest. Why the urgency? Why so many calls? Had she said anything yesterday? Why would he be so persistent? It was completely unlike him.

Is there any way he could have found out? No . . . that was impossible. Unless someone saw her here yesterday and called. . . . But they would have had to follow her out to Noah's. No one would have done that.

She had to call him now; no way to get around it. But she didn't want to, strangely. This was her time, and she wanted to spend it doing what she wanted. She hadn't planned on speaking to him until later, and for some reason she felt almost as if talking to him now would spoil the day. Besides, what was she going to say? How could she explain being out so late? A late dinner and then a walk? Maybe. Or a movie? Or . . .

"Miss?"

Almost noon, she thought. Where would he be? His office, probably. . . . No. In court, she suddenly realized, and immediately felt as if she'd been released from shackles. There was no way she could talk to him, even if she wanted to. She was surprised by her feelings. She shouldn't feel this way, she knew, and yet it didn't bother her. She looked at her watch, acting now.

"Is it really almost twelve?"

The manager nodded after looking at the clock. "Yes, a quarter till, actually."

"Unfortunately," she started, "he's in court right now and I can't reach him. If he does call again, could you tell him I'm shopping and that I'll try to call him later?"

"Of course," he answered. She could see the question in his eyes, though: *But where were you last night?* He had known exactly when she'd come in. Too late for a single woman in this small town, she was sure.

"Thank you," she said, smiling. "I'd appreciate it."

Two minutes later she was in her car, driving to Noah's, anticipating the day, largely unconcerned about the phone calls. Yesterday she would have been, and she wondered what that meant.

As she was driving over the drawbridge less than four minutes after she'd left the inn, Lon called from the courthouse.

Moving Water

Noah was sitting in his rocker, drinking sweet tea, listening for the car, when he finally heard it turn up the drive. He went around front and watched the car pull up and park beneath the oak tree again. Same spot as yesterday. Clem barked a greeting at her car door, tail wagging, and he saw Allie wave from inside the car.

She stepped out, patted Clem on the head while she cooed at her, then turned, smiling at Noah as he walked toward her. She looked more relaxed than yesterday, more confident, and again he felt a slight shock at seeing her. It was different from yesterday, though. Newer feelings now, not simply memories anymore. If anything, his attraction for her had grown stronger overnight, more intense, and it made him feel a little nervous in her presence.

98

Allie met him halfway, carrying a small bag in one hand. She surprised him by kissing him gently on the cheek, her free hand lingering at his waist after she pulled back.

"Hi," she said, radiance in her eyes, "where's the surprise?"

He relaxed a little, thanking God for that. "Not even a 'Good afternoon' or 'How was your night?'"

She smiled. Patience had never been one of her strongest attributes.

"Fine. Good afternoon. How was your night? And where's the surprise?"

He chuckled lightly, then paused. "Allie, I've got some bad news."

"What?"

"I was going to take you someplace, but with those clouds coming in, I'm not sure we should go."

"Why?"

"The storm. We'll be outside and might get wet. Besides, there might be lightning."

"It's not raining yet. How far is it?"

"Up the creek about a mile."

"And I've never been there before?"

"Not when it was like this."

She thought for a second while she looked around. When she spoke, her voice was determined.

"Then we'll go. I don't care if it rains."

"Are you sure?"

"Absolutely."

He looked at the clouds again, noting their approach. "Then we'd better go now," he said. "Can I bring that in for you?"

She nodded, handing her bag to him, and he jogged to the house and brought it inside, where he placed it on a chair in the living room. Then he grabbed some bread and put it in a bag, bringing it with him as he left the house.

They walked to the canoe, Allie beside him. A little closer than yesterday.

"What exactly is this place?"

"You'll see."

"You're not even going to give me a hint?"

"Well," he said, "do you remember when we took the canoe out and watched the sun come up?"

"I thought about it this morning. I remember it made me cry."

"What you're going to see today makes what you saw then seem ordinary."

"I guess I should feel special."

He took a few steps before responding.

"You are special," he finally said, and the way he said it made her wonder if he wanted to add something else. But he didn't, and Allie smiled a little before glancing away. As she did, she felt the wind in her face and noticed it had picked up since the morning.

They reached the dock a moment later. After tossing the bag in the canoe, Noah quickly checked to make sure he hadn't missed anything, then slid the canoe to the water.

"Can I do anything?"

"No, just get in."

After she climbed in, he pushed the canoe farther into the water, close to the dock. Then he gracefully stepped off the dock into the canoe, placing his feet carefully to prevent the canoe from capsizing. Allie was impressed by his agility, knowing that what he had done so quickly and easily was harder than it looked.

Allie sat at the front of the canoe, facing backward. He had said something about missing the view when he started to paddle, but she'd shaken her head, saying she was fine the way she was.

And it was true.

She could see everything she really wanted to see if she turned her head, but most of all she wanted to watch Noah. It was him she'd come to see, not the creek. His shirt was unbuttoned at the top, and she could see his chest muscles flex with every stroke. His sleeves were rolled up, too, and she could see the muscles in his arms bulging slightly. His muscles were well developed there from paddling every morning.

Artistic, she thought. There's something almost artistic about him when he does this. Something natural, as if being on the water were beyond his control, part of a gene passed on to him from some obscure hereditary pool. When she watched him, she was reminded of how the early explorers must have looked when they'd first discovered this area.

She couldn't think of anyone else who remotely resembled him. He was complicated, almost contradictory in so many ways, yet simple, a strangely erotic combination. On the surface he was a country boy, home from war, and he probably saw himself in those terms. Yet there was so much more to him. Perhaps it was the poetry that made him different, or perhaps it was the values his father had instilled in him, growing up. Either way, he seemed to savor life more fully than others appeared to, and that was what had first attracted her to him.

"What are you thinking?"

She felt her insides jump just a bit as Noah's voice brought her back to the present. She realized she hadn't said much since they'd started, and she appreciated the silence he had allowed her. He'd always been considerate like that.

"Good things," she answered quietly, and she saw in his eyes that he knew she was thinking about him. She liked the fact that he knew it, and she hoped he had been thinking about her as well.

She understood then that something was stirring within her, as it had so many years ago. Watching him, watching his body move, made her feel it. And as their eyes lingered for a second, she felt the heat in her neck and breasts, and she flushed, turning away before he noticed.

"How much farther?" she asked.

"Another half mile or so. Not any more than that."

A pause. Then, she said: "It's pretty out here. So clean. So quiet. It's almost like going back in time."

"In a way it is, I think. The creek flows from the forest. There's not a single farm between here and where it starts, and the water is pure as rain. It's probably as pure as it's ever been."

She leaned toward him. "Tell me, Noah, what do you remember most from the summer we spent together?"

"All of it."

"Anything in particular?"

"No," he said.

"You don't remember?"

He answered after a moment, quietly, seriously.

"No, it's not that. It's not what you're thinking. I was serious when I said 'all of it.' I can remember every moment we were together, and in each of them there was something wonderful. I can't really pick any one time that meant more than any other. The entire summer was perfect, the kind of summer everyone should have. How could I pick one moment over another?

"Poets often describe love as an emotion that we can't control, one that overwhelms logic and common sense. That's what it was like for me. I didn't plan on falling in love with you, and I doubt if you planned on falling in love with me.

But once we met, it was clear that neither of us could control what was happening to us. We fell in love, despite our differences, and once we did, something rare and beautiful was created. For me, love like that has happened only once, and that's why every minute we spent together has been seared in my memory. I'll never forget a single moment of it."

Allie stared at him. No one had ever said anything like that to her before. Ever. She didn't know what to say and stayed silent, her face hot.

"I'm sorry if I made you feel uncomfortable, Allie. I didn't mean to. But that summer has stayed with me and probably always will. I know it can't be the same between us, but that doesn't change the way I felt about you then."

She spoke quietly, feeling warm.

"It didn't make me uncomfortable, Noah. . . . It's just that I don't ever hear things like that. What you said was beautiful. It takes a poet to talk the way you do, and like I said, you're the only poet I've ever met."

Peaceful silence descended on them. An osprey cried somewhere in the distance. A mullet splashed near the bank. The paddle moved rhythmically, causing baffles that rocked the boat ever so slightly. The breeze had stopped, and the clouds grew blacker as the canoe moved toward some unknown destination.

Allie noticed it all, every sound, every thought. Her senses had come alive, invigorating her, and she felt her mind drifting through the last few weeks. She thought about the anxiety coming here had caused her. The shock at seeing the article, the sleepless nights, her short temper during daylight. Even yesterday she had been afraid and wanted to run away. The tension was gone now, every bit of it, replaced by something else, and she was glad about that as she rode in silence in the old red canoe.

She felt strangely satisfied that she'd come, pleased that Noah had turned into the type of man she'd thought he would, pleased that she would live forever with that knowledge. She had seen too many men in the past few years destroyed by war, or time, or even money. It took strength to hold on to inner passion, and Noah had done that.

This was a worker's world, not a poet's, and people would have a hard time understanding Noah. America was in full swing now, all the papers said so, and people were rushing forward, leaving behind the horrors of war. She understood the reasons, but they were rushing, like Lon, toward long hours and profits, neglecting the things that brought beauty to the world.

Who did she know in Raleigh who took time off to fix a house? Or read Whitman or Eliot, finding images in the mind, thoughts of the spirit? Or hunted dawn from the bow of a canoe? These weren't the things that drove society, but she felt they shouldn't be treated as unimportant. They made living worthwhile.

To her it was the same with art, though she had realized it only upon coming here. Or rather, remembered it. She had known it once before, and again she cursed herself for forgetting something as important as creating beauty. Painting was what she was meant to do, she was sure of that now. Her feelings this morning had confirmed it, and she knew that whatever happened, she was going to give it another shot. A fair shot, no matter what anyone said.

Would Lon encourage her painting? She remembered showing him one of her paintings a couple of months after they had first started going out. It was an abstract painting and was meant to inspire thought. In a way, it resembled the painting above Noah's fireplace, the one Noah understood completely, though it may have been a touch less passionate. Lon had stared at it, studied it almost, and then had asked her what it was supposed to be. She hadn't bothered to answer.

She shook her head then, knowing she wasn't being completely fair. She loved Lon, and always had, for other reasons. Though he wasn't Noah, Lon was a good man, the kind of man she'd always known she would marry. With Lon there would be no surprises, and there was comfort in knowing what the future would bring. He would be a kind husband to her, and she would be a good wife. She would have a home near friends and family, children, a respectable place in society. It was the kind of life she'd always expected to live, the kind of life she wanted to live. And though she wouldn't describe theirs as a passionate relationship, she had convinced herself long ago that this wasn't necessary to be fulfilled in a relationship, even with a person she intended to marry. Passion would fade in time, and things like companionship and compatibility would take its place. She and Lon had this, and she had assumed this was all she needed.

But now, as she watched Noah rowing, she questioned this basic assumption. He exuded sexuality in everything he did, everything he was, and she caught herself thinking about him in a way that an engaged woman shouldn't. She tried not to stare and glanced away often, but the easy way he moved his body made it hard to keep her eyes from him for long.

"Here we are," Noah said as he guided the canoe toward some trees near the bank.

Allie looked around, not seeing anything. "Where is it?"

"Here," he said again, pointing the canoe at an old tree that had fallen over, obscuring an opening almost completely hidden from view.

He guided the canoe around the tree, and both of them had to lower their heads to keep from bumping them.

"Close your eyes," he whispered, and Allie

did, bringing her hands to her face. She heard the baffles of the water and felt the movement of the canoe as he propelled it forward, away from the pull of the creek.

"Okay," he finally said after he'd stopped paddling. "You can open them now."

Swans and Storms

They sat in the middle of a small lake fed by the waters of Brices Creek. It wasn't large, maybe a hundred yards across, and she was surprised at how invisible it had been just moments before.

It was spectacular. Tundra swan and Canada geese literally surrounded them. Thousands of them. Birds floating so close together in some places that she couldn't see the water. From a distance, the groups of swans looked almost like icebergs.

"Oh, Noah," she finally said softly, "it's beautiful."

They sat in silence for a long while, watching the birds. Noah pointed out a group of chicks, recently hatched, following a pack of geese near the shore, struggling to keep up.

The air was filled with honking and chirping as Noah moved the canoe through the water. The birds ignored them for the most part. The only ones who seemed bothered were those forced to move when the canoe approached them. Allie reached out to touch the closest ones and felt their feathers ruffling under her fingers.

Noah brought out the bag of bread he'd brought earlier and handed it to Allie. She scattered the bread, favoring the little ones, laughing and smiling as they swam in circles, looking for food.

They stayed until thunder boomed in the distance—faint but powerful—and both of them knew it was time to leave.

Noah led them back to the current of the creek, paddling stronger than he had earlier. She was still amazed by what she had seen.

"Noah, what are they doing here?"

"I don't know. I know the swans from up north migrate to Lake Matamuskeet every winter, but I guess they came here this time. I don't know why. Maybe the early blizzard had something to do with it. Maybe they got off track or something. They'll find their way back, though."

"They won't stay?"

"I doubt it. They're driven by instinct, and this isn't their place. Some of the geese may winter here, but the swans will go back to Matamuskeet."

Noah paddled hard as dark clouds rolled

directly overhead. Soon rain began to fall, a light sprinkle at first, then gradually harder. Lightning . . . a pause . . . then thunder again. A little louder now. Maybe six or seven miles away. More rain as Noah began to paddle even harder, his muscles tightening with every stroke.

Thicker drops now.

Falling . . .

Falling with the wind . . .

Falling hard and thick . . . Noah rowing . . . racing the sky . . . still getting wet . . . cursing to himself . . . losing to Mother Nature . . .

The downpour was steady now, and Allie watched the rain fall diagonally from the sky, trying to defy gravity as it rode on westerly winds that whistled over the trees. The sky darkened a little more, and big heavy drops fell from the clouds. Hurricane drops.

Allie enjoyed the rain and leaned her head back for a moment to let it hit her face. She knew the front of her dress would soak through in a couple of minutes, but she didn't care. She did wonder, though, if he noticed, then thought he probably did.

She ran her hands through her hair, feeling its wetness. It felt wonderful, she felt wonderful, everything felt wonderful. Even through the rain, she could hear him breathing hard and the sound aroused her sexually in a way she hadn't felt in years.

A cloud burst directly above them, and the

rain began to come down even harder. Harder than she'd ever seen it. Allie looked upward and laughed, giving up any attempt at keeping dry, making Noah feel better. He hadn't known how she was feeling about it. Even though she'd made the decision to come, he doubted that she'd expected to be caught in a storm like this.

They reached the dock a couple of minutes later, and Noah moved in close enough for Allie to step out. He helped her up, then got out himself and dragged the canoe up the bank far enough not to drift away. Just in case, he tied it to the dock, knowing another minute in the rain wouldn't make any difference.

As he was tying the canoe, he looked up at Allie and stopped breathing for just a second. She was incredibly beautiful as she waited, watching him, completely comfortable in the rain. She didn't try to keep dry or hide herself, and he could see the outline of her breasts as they pressed through the fabric of the dress that clung tightly to her body. It wasn't a cold rain, but he could see her nipples erect and protruding, hard like little rocks. He felt his loins begin to stir and quickly turned away, embarrassed, muttering to himself, glad the rain muffled any sound of it. When he finished and stood, Allie took his hand in hers, surprising him. Despite the downpour, they didn't rush toward the house, and Noah imagined what it would be like to spend the night with her.

Allie, too, was wondering about him. She felt the warmth in his hands and wondered what it would be like to have them touch her body, feeling all of her, lingering slowly across her skin. Just thinking about it made her take a deep breath, and she felt her nipples begin to tingle and a new warmth between her legs.

She realized then that something had changed since she'd come here. And although she couldn't pinpoint the exact time—yesterday after dinner, or this afternoon in the canoe, or when they saw the swans, or maybe even now as they walked holding hands—she knew that she had fallen in love with Noah Taylor Calhoun again, and that maybe, just maybe, she had never stopped.

There was no uneasiness between them as they reached the door and both of them went inside, pausing in the foyer, clothes dripping.

"Did you bring a change of clothes?"

She shook her head, still feeling the roll of emotions within her, wondering if it showed on her face.

"I think I can find something here for you so you can get out of those clothes. It might be a little big, but it's warm."

"Anything," she said.

"I'll be back in a second."

Noah slipped off his boots, then ran up the stairs, descending a minute later. He had a pair of cotton pants and a long-sleeved shirt under one arm and some jeans with a blue shirt in the other.

"Here," he said, handing her the cotton pants and shirt. "You can change in the bedroom upstairs. There's a bathroom and towel up there too if you want to shower."

She thanked him with a smile and went up the stairs, feeling his eyes on her as she walked. She entered the bedroom and closed the door, then set the pants and shirt on his bed and peeled everything off. Naked, she went to his closet and found a hanger, put her dress, bra, and panties on it, and then went to hang it in the bathroom so it wouldn't drip on the hardwood floor. She felt a secret thrill at being naked in the same room he slept in.

She didn't want to shower after being in the rain. She liked the soft feeling on her skin, and it reminded her of how people used to live long ago. Naturally. Like Noah. She slipped on his clothes before looking at herself in the mirror. The pants were big, but tucking in the shirt helped, and she rolled up the bottoms just a little so they wouldn't drag. The neck was torn a little and it nearly hung off one shoulder, but she liked the way it looked on her anyway. She pulled the sleeves up almost to the elbows, went to the bureau, and slipped on some socks, then went to the bathroom to find a hairbrush.

She brushed her wet hair just enough to get out the snarls, letting it rest on her shoulders. Looking in the mirror, she wished she had brought a clasp or a couple of hairpins.

And a little more mascara. But what could she do? Her eyes still had a little of what she'd put on earlier, and she touched up with a washcloth, doing the best she could.

When she was finished, she checked herself in the mirror, feeling pretty despite everything, and went back down the stairs.

Noah was in the living room squatting before a fire, doing his best to coax it to life. He didn't see her come in, and she watched him as he worked. He had changed his clothes as well and looked good: his shoulders broad, wet hair hanging just over his collar, jeans tight.

He poked the fire, moving the logs, and added some more kindling. Allie leaned against the doorjamb, one leg crossed over the other, and continued to watch him. In a few minutes the fire had turned to flames, even and steady. He turned to the side to straighten the remaining unused logs and caught a glimpse of her out of the corner of his eye. He turned back to her quickly.

Even in his clothes she looked beautiful. After a moment he turned away shyly, going back to stacking the logs.

"I didn't hear you come in," he said, trying to sound casual.

"I know. You weren't supposed to." She knew what he had been thinking and felt a tinge of amusement at how young he seemed.

"How long have you been standing there?"

"A couple of minutes."

Noah brushed his hands on his pants, then pointed to the kitchen. "Can I get you some tea? I started the water while you were upstairs." Small talk, anything to keep his mind clear. But damn, the way she looked . . .

She thought for a second, saw the way he was looking at her, and felt the old instincts take over.

"Do you have anything stronger, or is it too early to drink?"

He smiled. "I have some bourbon in the pantry. Is that okay?"

"That sounds great."

He started toward the kitchen, and Allie watched him run his hand through his wet hair as he disappeared.

Thunder boomed loudly, and another downpour started. Allie could hear the roaring of the rain on the roof, could hear the snapping of logs as the flickering flames lit the room. She turned to the window and saw the gray sky flash lighter for just a second. Moments later, another boom of thunder. Close this time.

She took a quilt from the sofa and sat on the rug in front of the fire. Crossing her legs, she adjusted the quilt until she was comfortable and watched the dancing flames. Noah came back, saw what she had done, and went to sit beside her. He put down two glasses and poured some bourbon into each of them. Outside, the sky grew darker.

Thunder again. Loud. The storm in full fury,

winds whipping the rain in circles.

"It's quite a storm," Noah said as he watched the drops flow in vertical streams on the windows. He and Allie were close now, though not touching, and Noah watched her chest rise slightly with every breath, imagining the feel of her body once again before fighting it back.

"I like it," she said, taking a sip. "I've always liked thunderstorms. Even as a young girl."

"Why?" Saying anything, keeping his balance.

"I don't know. They just always seemed romantic to me."

She was quiet for a moment, and Noah watched the fire flicker in her emerald eyes. Then she said, "Do you remember sitting together and watching the storm a few nights before I left?"

"Of course."

"I used to think about it all the time after I went home. I always thought about how you looked that night. It was the way I always remembered you."

"Have I changed much?"

She took another sip of bourbon, feeling it warm her. She touched his hand as she answered.

"Not really. Not in the things that I remember. You're older, of course, with more life behind you, but you've still got the same gleam in your eye. You still read poetry and float on rivers. And you've still got a gentleness that not even the war could take away."

He thought about what she'd said and felt her

hand lingering on his, her thumb tracing slow circles.

"Allie, you asked me earlier what I remembered most about the summer. What do you remember?"

It was a while before she answered. Her voice seemed to come from somewhere else.

"I remember making love. That's what I remember most. You were my first, and it was more wonderful than I ever thought it would be."

Noah took a drink of bourbon, remembering, bringing back the old feelings again, then suddenly shook his head. This was already hard enough. She went on.

"I remember being so afraid beforehand that I was trembling, but at the same time being so excited. I'm glad you were the first. I'm glad we were able to share that."

"Me too."

"Were you as afraid as I was?"

Noah nodded without speaking, and she smiled at his honesty.

"I thought so. You were always shy like that. Especially in the beginning. I remember you had asked if I had a boyfriend, and when I said I did, you barely talked to me anymore."

"I didn't want to get between the two of you."

"You did, though, in the end, despite your professed innocence," she said, smiling. "And I'm glad you did."

"When did you finally tell him about us?"

"After I got home."

"Was it hard?"

"Not at all. I was in love with you."

She squeezed his hand, let go, and moved closer. She put her hand through his arm, cradling it, and rested her head on his shoulder. He could smell her, soft like the rain, warm. She spoke quietly:

"Do you remember walking home after the festival? I asked you if you wanted to see me again. You just nodded your head and didn't say a word. It wasn't too convincing."

"I'd never met anyone like you before. I couldn't help it. I didn't know what to say."

"I know. You could never hide anything. Your eyes always gave you away. You had the most wonderful eyes I'd ever seen."

She paused then, lifted her head from his shoulder, and looked directly at him. When she spoke, her voice was barely above a whisper. "I think I loved you more that summer than I ever loved anyone."

Lightning flashed again. In the quiet moments before the thunder, their eyes met as they tried to undo the fourteen years, both of them sensing a change since yesterday. When the thunder finally sounded, Noah sighed and turned from her, toward the windows.

"I wish you could have read the letters I wrote you," he said.

She didn't speak for a long while.

"It wasn't just up to you, Noah. I didn't tell you, but I wrote you a dozen letters after I got home. I just never sent them."

"Why?" Noah was surprised.

"I guess I was too afraid."

"Of what?"

"That maybe it wasn't as real as I thought it was. That maybe you forgot me."

"I would never do that. I couldn't even think it."

"I know that now. I can see it when I look at you. But back then, it was different. There was so much I didn't understand, things that a young girl's mind couldn't sort out."

"What do you mean?"

She paused, collecting her thoughts.

"When your letters never came, I didn't know what to think. I remember talking to my best friend about what happened that summer, and she said that you got what you wanted, and that she wasn't surprised that you wouldn't write. I didn't believe that you were that way, I never did, but hearing it and thinking about all our differences made me wonder if maybe the summer meant more to me than it had meant to you. . . . And then, while all this was going through my head, I heard from Sarah. She said that you had left New Bern."

"Fin and Sarah always knew where I was—"

She held up her hand to stop him. "I know, but I never asked. I assumed that you had left

New Bern to start a new life, one without me. Why else wouldn't you write? Or call? Or come see me?"

Noah looked away without answering, and she continued:

"I didn't know, and in time, the hurt began to fade and it was easier to just let it go. At least I thought it was. But in every boy I met in the next few years, I found myself looking for you, and when the feelings got too strong, I'd write you another letter. But I never sent them for fear of what I might find. By then, you'd gone on with your life and I didn't want to think about you loving someone else. I wanted to remember us like we were that summer. I didn't want to ever lose that."

She said it so sweetly, so innocently, that Noah wanted to kiss her when she finished. But he didn't. Instead he fought the urge and pushed it back, knowing it wasn't what she needed. Yet she felt so wonderful to him, touching him. . . .

"The last letter I wrote was a couple of years ago. After I met Lon, I wrote to your daddy to find out where you were. But it had been so long since I'd seen you, I wasn't even sure he'd still be there. And with the war . . ."

She trailed off, and they were quiet for a moment, both of them lost in thought. Lightning lit the sky again before Noah finally broke the silence.

"I wish you would have mailed it anyway."

"Why?"

"Just to hear from you. To hear what you've been up to."

"You might have been disappointed. My life isn't too exciting. Besides, I'm not exactly what you remembered."

"You're better than I remembered, Allie."

"You're sweet, Noah."

He almost stopped there, knowing that if he kept the words inside him, he could somehow keep control, the same control he had kept the past fourteen years. But something else had overtaken him now, and he gave in to it, hoping somehow, in some way, it would take them back to what they'd had so long ago.

"I'm not saying it because I'm sweet. I'm saying it because I love you now and I always have. More than you can imagine."

A log snapped, sending sparks up the chimney, and both of them noticed the smoldering remains, almost burned through. The fire needed another log, but neither of them moved.

Allie took another sip of bourbon and began to feel its effects. But it wasn't just the alcohol that made her hold Noah a little tighter and feel his warmth against her. Glancing out the window, she saw the clouds were almost black.

"Let me get the fire going again," Noah said, needing to think, and she released him. He went to the fireplace, opened the screen, and added a couple of logs. He used the poker to adjust the burning wood, making sure the new wood could catch easily.

The flame began to spread again, and Noah returned to her side. She snuggled up against him again, resting her head on his shoulder as she had before, not speaking, rubbing her hand lightly against his chest. Noah leaned closer and whispered in her ear.

"This reminds me of how we once were. When we were young."

She smiled, thinking the same thing, and they watched the fire and smoke, holding each other.

"Noah, you've never asked, but I want you to know something."

"What is it?"

Her voice was tender.

"There's never been another, Noah. You weren't just the first. You're the only man I've ever been with. I don't expect you to say the same thing, but I wanted to know."

Noah was silent as he turned away. She felt warmer as she watched the fire. Her hand ran over the muscles beneath his shirt, hard and firm as they leaned against each other.

She remembered when they'd held each other like this for what they'd thought would be the last time. They were sitting on a sea wall designed to hold back the waters of the Neuse River. She was crying because they might never see each other again, and she wondered how she could ever be happy again. Instead of answering, he pressed a note into her hand, which she read on the way home. She had saved it, occasionally reading all of it or sometimes just a part. One part she'd read at least a hundred times, and for some reason it ran through her head now. It said:

The reason it hurts so much to separate is because our souls are connected. Maybe they always have been and will be. Maybe we've lived a thousand lives before this one and in each of them we've found each other. And maybe each time, we've been forced apart for the same reasons. That means that this good-bye is both a good-bye for the past ten thousand years and a prelude to what will come.

When I look at you, I see your beauty and grace and know they have grown stronger with every life you have lived. And I know I have spent every life before this one searching for you. Not someone like you, but you, for your soul and mine must always come together. And then, for a reason neither of us understands, we've been forced to say good-bye.

I would love to tell you that everything will work out for us, and I promise to do all I can to make sure it does. But if we never meet again and this is truly good-bye, I know we will see each other again in another life. We will find each other again, and maybe the stars will have changed, and we will not only love each other in that time, but for all the times we've had before.

Could it be? she wondered. Could he be right? She had never completely discounted it, wanting to hold on to its promise in case it was true. The idea had helped her through many hard times. But sitting here now seemed to test the theory that they were destined to always be apart. Unless the stars had changed since they were last together.

And maybe they had, but she didn't want to look. Instead she leaned into him and felt the heat between them, felt his body, felt his arm tight around her. And her body began to tremble with the same anticipation she had felt the first time they were together.

It felt so right to be here. Everything felt right. The fire, the drinks, the storm—it couldn't have been more perfect. Like magic, it seemed, their years apart didn't matter anymore.

Lightning cut the sky outside. Fire danced on white-hot wood, spreading the heat. October rain sheeted itself against the windows, drowning out all other sounds.

They gave in then to everything they had fought the last fourteen years. Allie lifted her head off his shoulder, looked at him with hazy eyes, and Noah kissed her softly on the lips. She brought her hand to his face and touched his cheek, brushing it softly with her fingers. He leaned in slowly and kissed her again, still soft and tender, and she kissed back, feeling the years of separation dissolve into passion.

She closed her eyes and parted her lips as he ran his fingers up and down her arms, slowly, lightly. He kissed her neck, her cheek, her eyelids, and she felt the moisture of his mouth linger wherever his lips had touched. She took his hand and led it to her breasts, and a whimper rose in her throat as he gently touched them through the thin fabric of the shirt.

The world seemed dreamlike as she pulled back from him, the firelight setting her face aglow. Without speaking, she started to undo the buttons on his shirt. He watched her as she did it and listened to her soft breaths as she made her way downward. With each button he could feel her fingers brushing against his skin, and she smiled softly at him when she finally finished. He felt her slide her hands inside, touching him as lightly as possible, letting her hands explore his body. He was hot and she ran her hand over his slightly wet chest, feeling his hair between her fingers. Leaning in, she kissed his neck gently as she pulled the shirt over his shoulders, locking his arms behind his back. She lifted her head and allowed him to kiss her as he rolled his shoulders, freeing himself from the sleeves.

With that, he slowly reached for her. He lifted her shirt and ran his finger slowly across her belly before raising her arms and slipping it off. She felt short of breath as he lowered his head and kissed between her breasts and slowly ran his tongue up to her neck. His hands gently caressed her back, her arms, her shoulders, and she felt their heated bodies press together, skin to skin. He kissed her neck and nibbled gently as she lifted her hips and allowed him to pull off her bottoms. She reached for the snap on his jeans, undid it, and watched as he slipped them off as well. It was almost slow motion as their naked bodies finally came together, both of them trembling with the memory of what they had once shared together.

He ran his tongue along her neck while his hands moved over the smooth hot skin of her breasts, down her belly, past her navel, and up again. He was struck by her beauty. Her shimmering hair trapped the light and made it sparkle. Her skin was soft and beautiful, almost glowing in the firelight. He felt her hands on his back, beckoning him.

They lay back, close to the fire, and the heat made the air seem thick. Her back was slightly arched as he rolled atop her in one fluid motion. He was on all fours above her, his knees astride her hips. She lifted her head and kissed his chin and neck, breathing hard, licking his shoulders, and tasting the sweat that lingered on his body. She ran her hands through his hair as he held himself above her, his arm muscles hard from the exertion. With a little tempting frown, she pulled him closer, but he resisted. Instead he lowered himself and lightly rubbed his chest against her, and she felt her body respond with anticipation. He did this slowly, over and over, kissing every part of her body, listening as she made soft, whimpering sounds while he moved above her.

He did this until she couldn't take it anymore, and when they finally joined as one, she cried aloud and pressed her fingers hard into his back. She buried her face in his neck and felt him deep inside her, felt his strength and gentleness, felt his muscle and his soul. She moved rhythmically against him, allowing him to take her wherever he wanted, to the place she was meant to be.

She opened her eyes and watched him in the firelight, marveling at his beauty as he moved above her. She saw his body glisten with crystal sweat and watched as beads rolled down his chest and fell onto her like the rain outside. And with every drop, with every breath, she felt herself, every responsibility, every facet of her life, slipping away.

Their bodies reflected everything given, everything taken, and she was rewarded with a sensation she never knew existed. It went on and on, tingling throughout her body and warming her before finally subsiding, and she struggled to catch her breath while she trembled beneath him. But the moment it was over, another one started to build again, and she started to feel them in long sequences, one right after the next. By the time the rain had stopped and the sun had set, her body was exhausted but unwilling to stop the pleasure between them.

They spent the day in each other's arms, alternately making love by the fire and then holding each other as they watched the flames curl around the wood. Sometimes he recited one of his favorite poems as she lay beside him, and she would listen with her eyes closed and almost feel the words. Then, when they were ready, they would join again and he murmured words of love between kisses as they wrapped their arms around one another.

They went on throughout the evening, making up for their years apart, and slept in each other's arms that night. Occasionally he would wake up and look at her, her body spent and radiant, and feel as if everything were suddenly right in this world.

Once, when he was looking at her in the moments before daybreak, her eyes fluttered open and she smiled and reached up to touch his face. He put his fingers to her lips, gently, to keep her from speaking, and for a long time they just looked at one another.

When the lump in his throat subsided, he whispered to her, "You are the answer to every prayer I've offered. You are a song, a dream, a whisper, and I don't know how I could have lived without you for as long as I have. I love you, Allie, more than you can ever imagine. I always have, and I always will."

"Oh, Noah," she said, pulling him to her. She wanted him, needed him now more than ever, like nothing she'd ever known.

Courtrooms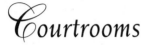

Later that morning, three men—two lawyers and the judge—sat in chambers while Lon finished speaking. It was a moment before the judge answered.

"It's an unusual request," he said, pondering the situation. "It seems to me the trial could very well end today. Are you saying this urgent matter can't wait until later this evening or tomorrow?"

"No, Your Honor, it can't," Lon answered almost too quickly. Stay relaxed, he told himself. Take a deep breath.

"And it has nothing to do with this case?"

"No, Your Honor. It's of a personal nature. I know it's out of the ordinary, but I really need to take care of it." Good, better.

The judge leaned back in his chair, evaluating

him for a moment. "Mr. Bates, how do you feel about this?"

He cleared his throat. "Mr. Hammond called me this morning and I've already spoken to my clients. They're willing to postpone until Monday."

"I see," the judge said. "And do you believe it is in your clients' best interests to do this?"

"I believe so," he said. "Mr. Hammond has agreed to reopen discussion on a certain matter not covered by this proceeding."

The judge looked hard at both of them and thought about it.

"I don't like it," he finally said, "not at all. But Mr. Hammond has never made a similar request before, and I assume the matter is very important to him."

He paused for effect, then looked to some papers on his desk. "I'll agree to adjourn until Monday. Nine o'clock sharp."

"Thank you, Your Honor," Lon said.

Two minutes later he was leaving the courthouse. He walked to the car he had parked directly across the street, got in, and began the drive to New Bern, his hands shaking.

An Unexpected Visitor

Noah made breakfast for Allie while she slept in the living room. Bacon, biscuits, and coffee, nothing spectacular. He set the tray beside her as she woke up, and as soon as they had finished eating, they made love again. It was relentless, a powerful confirmation of what they had shared the day before. Allie arched her back and cried out fiercely in the final tidal wave of sensations, then wrapped her arms around him as they breathed in unison, exhausted.

They showered together, and afterward Allie put on her dress, which had dried overnight. She spent the morning with Noah. Together they fed Clem and checked the windows to make sure no damage had been done in the storm. Two pine trees had blown over, though neither had caused much damage, and a few shingles had blown off the shed, but other than that, the property had escaped pretty much unscathed.

He held her hand most of the morning and the two talked easily, but sometimes he would stop speaking and just stare at her. When he did, she felt as though she should say something, but nothing meaningful ever came into her head. Lost in thought, she usually just kissed him.

A little before noon, Noah and Allie went in to prepare lunch. Both of them were starving again because they hadn't eaten much the day before. Using what he had on hand, they fried some chicken and baked another batch of biscuits, and the two of them ate on the porch, serenaded by a mockingbird.

While they were inside doing the dishes, they heard a knock at the door. Noah left Allie in the kitchen.

Knock again.

"I'm coming," Noah said.

Knock, knock. Louder.

He approached the door.

Knock, knock.

"I'm coming," he said again as he opened the door.

"Oh, my God."

He stared for a moment at a beautiful woman in her early fifties, a woman he would have recognized anywhere.

Noah couldn't speak.

"Hello, Noah," she finally said.

Noah said nothing.

"May I come in?" she asked, her voice steady, revealing nothing.

He stammered out a reply as she walked past him, stopping just before the stairs.

"Who is it?" Allie shouted from the kitchen, and the woman turned at the sound of her voice.

"It's your mother," Noah finally answered, and immediately after he said it, he heard the sound of breaking glass.

"I knew you would be here," Anne Nelson said to her daughter as the three of them sat around the coffee table in the living room.

"How could you be so sure?"

"You're my daughter. One day when you have kids of your own, you'll know the answer." She smiled, but her manner was stiff, and Noah imagined how difficult this must be for her. "I saw the article, too, and I saw your reaction. I also saw how tense you've been during the last couple of weeks, and when you said you were going shopping near the coast, I knew exactly what you meant."

"What about Daddy?"

Anne Nelson shook her head. "No, I didn't tell your father or anyone else about it. Nor did I tell anyone where I was going today."

The table was silent for a moment as they wondered what was coming next, but Anne remained quiet.

"Why did you come?" Allie finally asked.

Her mother raised an eyebrow. "I thought I would be the one to ask that question."

Allie paled.

"I came because I had to," her mother said, "which I'm sure is the same reason you came. Am I right?"

Allie nodded.

Anne turned to Noah. "These last couple of days must have been full of surprises."

"Yes," he answered simply, and she smiled at him.

"I know you don't think so, but I always liked you, Noah. I just didn't think you were right for my daughter. Can you understand that?"

He shook his head as he answered, his tone serious. "No, not really. It wasn't fair to me, and it wasn't fair to Allie. Otherwise she wouldn't be here."

She watched him as he answered, but she said nothing. Allie, sensing an argument, cut in:

"What do you mean when you say you had to come? Don't you trust me?"

Anne turned back to her daughter. "This has nothing to do with trust. This has to do with Lon. He called the house last night to talk to me about Noah, and he's on his way here right now. He seemed very upset. I thought you'd want to know."

Allie inhaled sharply. "He's on his way?"

"As we speak. He arranged to have the trial

postponed until next week. If he's not in New Bern yet, he's close."

"What did you say to him?"

"Not much. But he knew. He had it all figured out. He remembered my telling him about Noah a long time ago."

Allie swallowed hard. "Did you tell him I was here?"

"No. And I won't. That's between you and him. But knowing him, I'm sure he'll find you here if you stay. All it takes is a couple of phone calls to the right people. After all, I was able to find you."

Allie, though obviously worried, smiled at her mother. "Thank you," she said, and her mother reached for her hand.

"I know we've had our differences, Allie, and that we haven't seen eye to eye on everything. I'm not perfect, but I did the best I could with raising you. I'm your mother and I always will be. That means I'll always love you."

Allie was silent for a moment, then: "What should I do?"

"I don't know, Allie. That's up to you. But I would think about it. Think about what you really want."

Allie turned away, her eyes reddening. A moment later a tear drifted down her cheek.

"I don't know. . . ," she trailed off, and her mother squeezed her hand. Anne looked at Noah, who had been sitting with his head down, listening carefully. As if on cue, he returned her gaze, nodded, and left the room.

When he was gone, Anne whispered, "Do you love him?"

"Yes, I do," Allie answered softly, "very much."

"Do you love Lon?"

"Yes, I do. I love him, too. Dearly, but in a different way. He doesn't make me feel the way Noah does."

"No one will ever do that," her mother said, and she released Allie's hand.

"I can't make this decision for you, Allie, this one's all yours. I want you to know, though, that I love you. And I always will. I know that doesn't help, but it's all I can do."

She reached in her pocketbook and removed a bundle of letters held together with string, the envelopes old and slightly yellowed.

"These are the letters that Noah wrote you. I never threw them away, and they haven't been opened. I know I shouldn't have kept them from you, and I'm sorry for that. But I was just trying to protect you. I didn't realize . . ."

Allie took them and ran her hand over them, shocked.

"I should go, Allie. You've got some decisions to make, and you don't have much time. Do you want me to stay in town?"

Allie shook her head. "No, this is up to me."

Anne nodded and watched her daughter for a

moment, wondering. Finally she stood, went around the table, leaned over, and kissed her daughter on the cheek. She could see the question in her daughter's eyes as Allie stood from the table and embraced her.

"What are you going to do?" her mother asked, pulling back. There was a long pause.

"I don't know," Allie finally answered. They stood together for another minute, just holding each other.

"Thanks for coming," Allie said. "I love you."

"I love you, too."

On her way out the door, Allie thought that she heard her mother whisper, "Follow your heart," but she couldn't be sure.

Crossroads

Noah opened the door for Anne Nelson as she went out.

"Good-bye, Noah," she said quietly. He nodded without speaking. There wasn't anything else to say; they both knew that. She turned from him and left, closing the door behind her. Noah watched her walk to her car, get in, and drive away without looking back. She was a strong woman, he thought to himself, and he knew where Allie got it from.

Noah peeked in the living room, saw Allie sitting with her head down, then went to the back porch, knowing that she needed to be alone. He sat quietly in his rocker and watched the water drifting by as the minutes passed.

After what seemed like an eternity he heard the back door open. He didn't turn to look at her just then—for some reason he couldn't—and he listened as she sat in the chair beside him.

"I'm sorry," Allie said. "I had no idea this would happen."

Noah shook his head. "Don't be sorry. We both knew it was coming in some form or another."

"It's still hard."

"I know." He finally turned to her, reaching for her hand. "Is there anything I can do to make it easier?"

She shook her head. "No. Not really. I have to do this alone. Besides, I'm not sure what I'm going to say to him yet." She looked down and her voice became softer and a little more distant, as if she were talking to herself. "I guess it depends on him and how much he knows. If my mother was right, he may have suspicions, but he doesn't know anything for sure."

Noah felt a tightness in his stomach. When he finally spoke his voice was steady, but she could hear the pain in it.

"You're not going to tell him about us, are you?"

"I don't know. I really don't. While I was in the living room, I kept asking myself what I really wanted in my life." She squeezed his hand. "And do you know what the answer was? The answer was that I wanted two things. First, I want you. I want us. I love you and I always have."

She took a deep breath before going on.

"But I also want a happy ending without hurting anyone. And I know that if I stayed, people would be hurt. Especially Lon. I wasn't lying when I told you that I love him. He doesn't make me feel the same way you do, but I care for him, and this wouldn't be fair to him. But staying here would also hurt my family and friends. I would be betraying everyone I know. . . . I don't know if I can do that."

"You can't live your life for other people. You've got to do what's right for you, even if it hurts some people you love."

"I know," she said, "but no matter what I choose I have to live with it. Forever. I have to be able to go forward and not look back anymore. Can you understand that?"

He shook his head and tried to keep his voice steady. "Not really. Not if it means losing you. I can't do that again."

She didn't say anything but lowered her head. Noah went on:

"Could you really leave me without looking back?"

She bit her lip as she answered. Her voice was beginning to crack. "I don't know. Probably not."

"Would that be fair to Lon?"

She didn't answer right away. Instead she stood, wiped her face, and walked to the edge of the porch where she leaned against the post. She crossed her arms and watched the water before answering quietly.

"No."

"It doesn't have to be like this, Allie," he said. "We're adults now, we have the choice we didn't have before. We're meant to be together. We always have been."

He walked to her side and put his hand on her shoulder. "I don't want to live the rest of my life thinking about you and dreaming of what might have been. Stay with me, Allie."

Tears began to fill her eyes. "I don't know if I can," she finally whispered.

"You can. Allie . . . I can't live my life happily knowing you're with someone else. That would kill a part of me. What we have is rare. It's too beautiful to just throw it away."

She didn't respond. After a moment he gently turned her toward him, took her hands, and stared at her, willing her to look at him. Allie finally faced him with moist eyes. After a long silence, Noah brushed the tears from her cheeks with his fingers, a look of tenderness on his face. His voice caught as he saw what her eyes were telling him.

"You're not going to stay, are you?" He smiled weakly. "You want to, but you can't."

"Oh, Noah," she said as the tears began again, "please try to understand. . . . "

He shook his head to stop her.

"I know what you're trying to say—I can see

it in your eyes. But I don't want to understand it, Allie. I don't want it to end this way. I don't want it to end at all. But if you leave, we both know we'll never see each other again."

She leaned into him and began to cry harder as Noah fought back his own tears.

He wrapped his arms around her.

"Allie, I can't force you to stay with me. But no matter what happens in my life, I'll never forget these last couple of days with you. I've been dreaming about this for years."

He kissed her gently, and they embraced as they had when she first got out of her car two days ago. Finally Allie let him go and wiped her tears.

"I have to get my things, Noah."

He didn't go inside with her. Instead he sat down in the rocker, spent. He watched her go into the house and listened as the sound of her movements faded into nothing. She emerged from the house minutes later with everything she'd brought and walked toward him with her head down. She handed him the drawing she had done yesterday morning. As he took it, he noticed that she hadn't stopped crying.

"Here, Noah. I made this for you."

Noah took the drawing and unrolled it slowly, careful not to tear it.

There were dual images, one overlapping the other. The image in the foreground, which occupied most of the page, was a picture of how he looked now, not fourteen years ago. Noah noticed that she had penciled in every detail of his face, including the scar. It was almost as if she'd copied it from a recent photograph.

The second image was that of the front of the house. The detail there was also incredible, as if she had sketched it while sitting beneath the oak tree.

"It's beautiful, Allie. Thank you." He attempted a smile. "I told you that you were an artist." She nodded, her face cast downward, her lips pressed together. It was time for her to go.

They walked to her car slowly, without speaking. When they reached it, Noah embraced her again until he could feel the tears welling up in his own eyes. He kissed her lips and both cheeks, then with his finger softly brushed the places he'd kissed.

"I love you, Allie."

"I love you, too."

Noah opened her car door, and they kissed one more time. Then she slid behind the wheel, never taking her eyes from him. She put the packet of letters and the pocketbook next to her on the seat and fumbled for the keys, then turned the ignition. It started easily, and the engine began to turn over impatiently. It was almost time.

Noah pushed her door closed with both hands, and Allie rolled down the window. She could see the muscles in his arms, the easy smile, the tanned face. She reached out her hand and Noah took it for just a moment, moving his fingers softly against her skin.

"Stay with me," Noah mouthed without sound, and this for some reason hurt more than Allie would have expected. The tears began to fall hard now, but she couldn't speak. Finally, reluctantly, she looked away and pulled her hand from his. She put the car in gear and eased the pedal down just a bit. If she didn't leave now, she never would. Noah backed up just a bit as the car started to roll away.

He fell into an almost trancelike state as he felt the reality of the situation. He watched the car roll slowly forward; he heard the gravel crunching under the wheels. Slowly the car began to turn from him, toward the road that would take her back to town. Leaving—she was leaving!—and Noah felt dizzy at the sight.

Edging forward . . . past him now . . .

She waved one last time without smiling before she began to accelerate, and he waved back weakly. "Don't go!" he wanted to shout as the car moved farther away. But he didn't say anything, and a minute later the car was gone and the only remaining signs of her were the tracks that her car had left behind.

He stood there without moving for a long time. As quickly as she had come, she was gone. Forever this time. Forever.

He closed his eyes then and watched her leave

once more, her car moving steadily away from him, taking his heart with her.

But, like her mother, he realized sadly, she never looked back.

A Letter from Yesterday

Driving with tears in her eyes was difficult, but she went on anyway, hoping that instinct would take her back to the inn. She kept the window rolled down, thinking the fresh air might help clear her mind, but it didn't seem to help. Nothing would help.

She was tired, and she wondered if she would have the energy she needed to talk to Lon. And what was she going to say? She still had no idea but hoped that something would come to her when the time came.

It would have to.

By the time she reached the drawbridge that led to Front Street, she had herself a little more under control. Not completely, but well enough, she thought, to talk to Lon. At least she hoped so.

Traffic was light, and she had time to watch

strangers going about their business as she drove through New Bern. At a gas station, a mechanic was looking under the hood of a new automobile while a man, presumably its owner, stood beside him. Two women were pushing baby carriages just outside Hoffman-Lane, chatting between themselves while they window-shopped. In front of Hearns Jewelers, a well-dressed man walked briskly, carrying a briefcase.

She made another turn and saw a young man unloading groceries from a truck that blocked part of the street. Something about the way he held himself, or the way he moved, reminded her of Noah harvesting crabs at the end of the dock.

She saw the inn just up the street while she was stopped at a red light. She took a deep breath when the light turned green and drove slowly until she reached the parking lot that the inn shared with a couple of other businesses. She turned in and saw Lon's car sitting in the first spot. Although the one next to it was open, she passed it and picked a spot a little farther from the entrance.

She turned the key, and the engine stopped promptly. Next she reached into the glove compartment for a mirror and brush, finding both sitting on top of a map of North Carolina. Looking at herself, she saw her eyes were still red and puffy. Like yesterday after the rain, as she examined her reflection she was sorry she didn't have any makeup, though she doubted it would help much now. She tried pulling her hair back on one side, tried both sides, then finally gave up.

She reached for her pocketbook, opened it, and once again looked at the article that had brought her here. So much had happened since then; it was hard to believe it had been only three weeks. It felt impossible to her that she had arrived only the day before yesterday. It seemed like a lifetime since her dinner with Noah.

Starlings chirped in the trees around her. The clouds had begun to break up now, and Allie could see blue in between patches of white. The sun was still shaded, but she knew it would only be a matter of time. It was going to be a beautiful day.

It was the kind of day she would have liked to spend with Noah, and as she was thinking about him, she remembered the letters her mother had given her and reached for them.

She untied the packet and found the first letter he had written her. She began to open it, then stopped because she could imagine what was in it. Something simple, no doubt—things he'd done, memories of the summer, perhaps some questions. After all, he probably expected an answer from her. Instead she reached for the last letter he'd written, the one on the bottom of the stack. The good-bye letter. This one interested her far more than the others. How had he said it? How would she have said it?

The envelope was thin. One, maybe two pages. Whatever he had written wasn't too long. First, she turned it over and checked the back. No name, just a street address in New Jersey. She held her breath as she used her fingernail to pry it open.

Unfolding it, she saw it was dated March 1935.

Two and a half years without a reply.

She imagined him sitting at an old desk, crafting the letter, somehow knowing this was the end, and she saw what she thought were tearstains on the paper. Probably just her imagination.

She straightened the page and began to read in the soft white sunlight that shone through the window.

> *My dearest Allie,*
> *I don't know what to say anymore except that I couldn't sleep last night because I knew that it is over between us. It is a different feeling for me, one that I never expected, but looking back, I suppose it couldn't have ended another way.*
> *You and I were different. We came from different worlds, and yet you were the one who taught me the value of love. You showed me what it was like to care for another, and I am a better man because of it. I don't want you to ever forget that.*

I am not bitter because of what has happened. On the contrary. I am secure in knowing that what we had was real, and I am happy we were able to come together for even a short period of time. And if, in some distant place in the future, we see each other in our new lives, I will smile at you with joy, and remember how we spent a summer beneath the trees, learning from each other and growing in love. And maybe, for a brief moment, you'll feel it too, and you'll smile back, and savor the memories we will always share together.

I love you, Allie.

Noah

She read the letter again, more slowly this time, then read it a third time before she put it back into the envelope. Once more, she imagined him writing it, and for a moment she debated reading another, but she knew she couldn't delay any longer. Lon was waiting for her.

Her legs felt weak as she stepped out of the car. She paused and took a deep breath, and as she started across the parking lot, she realized she still wasn't sure what she was going to say to him.

And the answer didn't finally come until she reached the door and opened it and saw Lon standing in the lobby.

Winter for Two

The story ends there, so I close the notebook, remove my glasses, and wipe my eyes. They are tired and bloodshot, but they have not failed me so far. They will soon, I am sure. Neither they nor I can go on forever. I look to her now that I have finished, but she does not look back. Instead she is staring out the window at the courtyard, where friends and family meet.

My eyes follow hers, and we watch it together. In all these years the daily pattern has not changed. Every morning, an hour after breakfast, they begin to arrive. Young adults, alone or with family, come to visit those who live here. They bring photographs and gifts and either sit on the benches or stroll along the tree-lined paths designed to give a sense of nature. Some will stay for the day, but most leave after a few hours, and when they do, I always feel sadness for those they've left behind. I wonder sometimes what my friends think as they see their loved ones driving off, but I know it's not my business. And I do not ever ask them because I've learned that we're all entitled to have our secrets.

But soon, I will tell you some of mine.

I place the notebook and magnifier on the table beside me, feeling the ache in my bones as I do so, and I realize once again how cold my body is. Even reading in the morning sun does nothing to help it. This does not surprise me anymore, though, for my body makes its own rules these days.

I'm not completely unfortunate, however. The people who work here know me and my faults and do their best to make me more comfortable. They have left me hot tea on the end table, and I reach for it with both hands. It is an effort to pour a cup, but I do so because the tea is needed to warm me and I think the exertion will keep me from completely rusting away. But I am rusted now, no doubt about it. Rusted as a junked car twenty years in the Everglades.

I have read to her this morning, as I do every morning, because it is something I must do. Not for duty—although I suppose a case could be made for this—but for another, more romantic, reason. I wish I could explain it more fully right now, but it's still early, and talking about romance isn't really possible before lunch any-more, at least not for me. Besides, I have no idea how it's going to turn out, and to be honest, I'd rather not get my hopes up.

We spend each and every day together now, but our nights are spent alone. The doctors tell me that I'm not allowed to see her after dark. I understand the reasons completely, and though I agree with them, I sometimes break the rules. Late at night when my mood is right, I will sneak from my room and go to hers and watch her while she sleeps. Of this she knows nothing. I'll come in and see her breathe and know that had it not been for her, I would never have married. And when I look at her face, a face I know bet-ter than my own, I know that I have meant as much or more to her. And that means more to me than I could ever hope to explain.

Sometimes, when I am standing there, I think about how lucky I am to have been married to her for almost forty-nine years. Next month it will be that long. She heard me snore for the first forty-five, but since then we have slept in sepa-rate rooms. I do not sleep well without her. I toss and turn and yearn for her warmth and lie there most of the night, eyes open wide, watching the shadows dance across the ceilings like tumble-weeds rolling across the desert. I sleep two hours if I am lucky, and still I wake before dawn. This makes no sense to me.

Soon, this will all be over. I know this. She

does not. The entries in my diary have become shorter and take little time to write. I keep them simple now, since most of my days are the same. But tonight I think I will copy a poem that one of the nurses found for me and thought I would enjoy. It goes like this:

> I ne'er was struck before that hour
> With love so sudden and so sweet,
> Her face it bloomed like a sweet flower
> And stole my heart away complete.

Because our evenings are our own, I have been asked to visit the others. Usually I do, for I am the reader and I am needed, or so I am told. I walk the halls and choose where to go because I am too old to devote myself to a schedule, but deep down I always know who needs me. They are my friends, and when I push open their doors, I see rooms that look like mine, always semidarkened, illuminated only by the lights of *Wheel of Fortune* and Vanna's teeth. The furniture is the same for everyone, and the TVs blare because no one can hear well anymore.

Men or women, they smile at me when I enter and speak in whispers as they turn off their sets. "I'm so glad you've come," they say, and then they ask about my wife. Sometimes I tell them. I might tell them of her sweetness and her charm and describe how she taught me to see the world for the beautiful place it is. Or I tell them of our early years together and explain how we had all we needed when we held each other under starry southern skies. On special occasions I whisper of our adventures together, of art shows in New York and Paris or the rave reviews from critics writing in languages I do not understand. Mostly, though, I smile and I tell them that she is the same, and they turn from me, for I know they do not want me to see their faces. It reminds them of their own mortality. So I sit with them and read to lessen their fears.

> Be composed—be at ease with me . . .
> Not till the sun excludes you do I exclude
>   you,
> Not till the waters refuse to glisten for you
>   and the leaves to rustle for you, do my
>   words refuse to glisten and rustle for
>   you.

And I read, to let them know who I am.

> I wander all night in my vision, . . .
> Bending with open eyes over the shut eyes
>   of sleepers,
> Wandering and confused, lost to myself,
>   ill-assorted, contradictory,
> Pausing, gazing, bending, and stopping.

If she could, my wife would accompany me on my evening excursions, for one of her many loves was poetry. Thomas, Whitman, Eliot, Shakespeare, and King David of the Psalms. Lovers of words, makers of language. Looking back, I am surprised by my passion for it, and sometimes I even regret it now. Poetry brings great beauty to life, but also great sadness, and I'm not sure it's a fair exchange for someone my age. A man should enjoy other things if he can; he should spend his final days in the sun. Mine will be spent by a reading lamp.

I shuffle toward her and sit in the chair beside her bed. My back aches when I sit. I must get a new cushion for this chair, I remind myself for the hundredth time. I reach for her hand and take it, bony and fragile. It feels nice. She responds with a twitch, and gradually her thumb begins to softly rub my finger. I do not speak until she does; this I have learned. Most days I sit in silence until the sun goes down, and on days like those I know nothing about her.

Minutes pass before she finally turns to me. She is crying. I smile and release her hand, then reach in my pocket. I take out a handkerchief and wipe at her tears. She looks at me as I do so, and I wonder what she is thinking.

"That was a beautiful story."

A light rain begins to fall. Little drops tap gently on the window. I take her hand again. It is going to be a good day, a very good day. A magical day. I smile, I can't help it.

"Yes, it is," I tell her.

"Did you write it?" she asks. Her voice is like a whisper, a light wind flowing though the leaves.

"Yes," I answer.

She turns toward the nightstand. Her medicine is in a little cup. Mine too. Little pills, colors like a rainbow so we won't forget to take them. They bring mine here now, to her room, even though they're not supposed to.

"I've heard it before, haven't I?"

"Yes," I say again, just as I do every time on days like these. I have learned to be patient.

She studies my face. Her eyes are as green as ocean waves.

"It makes me feel less afraid," she says.

"I know." I nod, rocking my head softly.

She turns away, and I wait some more. She releases my hand and reaches for her water glass. It is on her nightstand, next to the medicine. She takes a sip.

"Is it a true story?" She sits up a little in her bed and takes another drink. Her body is still strong. "I mean, did you know these people?"

"Yes," I say again. I could say more, but usually I don't. She is still beautiful. She asks the obvious:

"Well, which one did she finally marry?"

I answer: "The one who was right for her."

"Which one was that?"

I smile. "You'll know," I say quietly, "by the end of the day. You'll know."

She does not know what to think about this but does not question me further. Instead she begins to fidget. She is thinking of a way to ask me another question, though she isn't sure how to do it. Instead she chooses to put it off for a moment and reaches for one of the little paper cups.

"Is this mine?"

"No, this one is," and I reach over and push her medicine toward her. I cannot grab it with my fingers. She takes it and looks at the pills. I can tell by the way she is looking at them that she has no idea what they are for. I use both hands to pick up my cup and dump the pills into my mouth. She does the same. There is no fight today. That makes it easy. I raise my cup in a mock toast and wash the gritty flavor from my mouth with my tea. It is getting colder. She swallows on faith and washes them down with more water.

A bird starts to sing outside the window, and we both turn our heads. We sit quietly for a while, enjoying something beautiful together. Then it is lost, and she sighs.

"I have to ask you something else," she says.

"Whatever it is, I'll try to answer."

"It's hard, though."

She does not look at me, and I cannot see her eyes. This is how she hides her thoughts. Some things never change.

"Take your time," I say. I know what she will ask.

Finally she turns to me and looks into my eyes. She offers a gentle smile, the kind you share with a child, not a lover.

"I don't want to hurt your feelings because you've been so nice to me, but . . ."

I wait. Her words will hurt me. They will tear a piece from my heart and leave a scar.

"Who are you?"

We have lived at Creekside Extended Care Facility for three years now. It was her decision to come here, partly because it was near our home, but also because she thought it would be easier for me. We boarded up our home because neither of us could bear to sell it, signed some papers, and just like that we received a place to live and die in exchange for some of the freedom for which we had worked a lifetime.

She was right to do this, of course. There is no way I could have made it alone, for sickness has come to us, both of us. We are in the final minutes in the day of our lives, and the clock is ticking. Loudly. I wonder if I am the only one who can hear it.

A throbbing pain courses through my fingers, and it reminds me that we have not held hands with fingers interlocked since we moved here. I am sad about this, but it is my fault, not hers. It is arthritis in the worst form, rheumatoid and advanced. My hands are misshapen and grotesque now, and they throb during most of my waking hours. I look at them and want them gone, amputated, but then I would not be able to do the little things I must do. So I use my claws, as I call them sometimes, and every day I take her hands despite the pain, and I do my best to hold them because that is what she wants me to do.

Although the Bible says man can live to be 120, I don't want to, and I don't think my body would make it even if I did. It is falling apart, dying one piece at a time, steady erosion on the inside and at the joints. My hands are useless, my kidneys are beginning to fail, and my heart rate is decreasing every month. Worse, I have cancer again, this time of the prostate. This is my third bout with the unseen enemy, and it will take me eventually, though not till I say it is time. The doctors are worried about me, but I am not. I have no time for worry in this twilight of my life.

Of our five children, four are still living, and though it is hard for them to visit, they come often, and for this I am thankful. But even when they aren't here, they come alive in my mind every day, each of them, and they bring to mind the smiles and tears that come with raising a family. A dozen pictures line the walls of my room. They are my heritage, my contribution to the world. I am very proud. Sometimes I wonder what my wife thinks of them as she dreams, or if she thinks of them at all, or if she even dreams. There is so much about her I don't understand anymore.

I wonder what my daddy would think of my life and what he would do if he were me. I have not seen him for fifty years and he is now but a shadow in my thoughts. I cannot picture him clearly anymore; his face is darkened as if a light shines from behind him. I am not sure if this is due to a failing memory or simply the passage of time. I have only one picture of him, and this too has faded. In another ten years it will be gone and so will I, and his memory will be erased like a message in the sand. If not for my diaries, I would swear I had lived only half as long as I have. Long periods of my life seem to have vanished. And even now I read the passages and wonder who I was when I wrote them, for I cannot remember the events of my life. There are times I sit and wonder where it all has gone.

"My name," I say, "is Duke." I have always been a John Wayne fan.

"Duke," she whispers to herself, "Duke." She thinks for a moment, her forehead wrinkled, her eyes serious.

"Yes," I say, "I'm here for you." And always will be, I think to myself.

She flushes with my answer. Her eyes become wet and red, and tears begin to fall. My heart aches for her, and I wish for the thousandth time that there was something I could do. She says:

"I'm sorry. I don't understand anything that's happening to me right now. Even you. When I listen to you talk I feel like I should know you, but I don't. I don't even know my name."

She wipes at her tears and says, "Help me, Duke, help me remember who I am. Or at least, who I was. I feel so lost."

I answer from my heart, but I lie to her about her name. As I have about my own. There is a reason for this.

"You are Hannah, a lover of life, a strength to those who shared in your friendships. You are a dream, a creator of happiness, an artist who has touched a thousand souls. You've led a full life and wanted for nothing because your needs are spiritual and you have only to look inside you. You are kind and loyal, and you are able to see beauty where others do not. You are a teacher of wonderful lessons, a dreamer of better things."

I stop for a moment and catch my breath. Then, "Hannah, there is no reason to feel lost, for:

> Nothing is ever really lost, or can be lost,
> No birth, identity, form—no object of the
>   world,
> Nor life, nor force, nor any visible thing; . . .
> The body, sluggish, aged, cold—the embers
>   left from earlier fires,
>   . . . shall duly flame again;"

She thinks about what I have said for a moment. In the silence, I look toward the window and notice that the rain has stopped now. Sunlight is beginning to filter into her room. She asks:

"Did you write that?"

"No, that was Walt Whitman."

"Who?"

"A lover of words, a shaper of thoughts."

She does not respond directly. Instead she stares at me for a long while, until our breathing coincides. In. Out. In. Out. In. Out. Deep breaths. I wonder if she knows I think she's beautiful.

"Would you stay with me a while?" she finally asks.

I smile and nod. She smiles back. She reaches for my hand, takes it gently, and pulls it to her waist. She stares at the hardened knots that deform my fingers and caresses them gently. Her hands are still those of an angel.

"Come," I say as I stand with great effort, "let's go for a walk. The air is crisp and the goslings are waiting. It's beautiful today." I am staring at her as I say these last few words.

She blushes. It makes me feel young again.

She was famous, of course. One of the best southern painters of the twentieth century, some said, and I was, and am, proud of her. Unlike me, who struggled to write even the simplest of verses, my wife could create beauty as easily as the Lord created the earth. Her paintings are in museums around the world, but I have kept only two for myself. The first one she ever gave me and the last one. They hang in my room, and late at night I sit and stare and sometimes cry when I look at them. I don't know why.

And so the years passed. We led our lives, working, painting, raising children, loving each other. I see photos of Christmases, family trips, of graduations and of weddings. I see grandchildren and happy faces. I see photos of us, our hair growing whiter, the lines in our faces deeper. A lifetime that seems so typical, yet uncommon.

We could not foresee the future, but then who can? I do not live now as I expected to. And what did I expect? Retirement. Visits with the grandchildren, perhaps more travel. She always loved to travel. I thought that perhaps I would start a hobby, what I did not know, but possibly shipbuilding. In bottles. Small, detailed, impossible to consider now with my hands. But I am not bitter.

Our lives can't be measured by our final years, of this I am sure, and I guess I should have known what lay ahead in our lives. Looking back, I suppose it seems obvious, but at first I thought her confusion understandable and not unique. She would forget where she placed her keys, but who has not done that? She would forget a neighbor's name, but not someone we knew well or with whom we socialized. Sometimes she would write the wrong year when she made out her checks, but again I dismissed it as simple mistakes that one makes when thinking of other things.

It was not until the more obvious events occurred that I began to suspect the worst. An iron in the freezer, clothes in the dishwasher, books in the oven. Other things, too. But the day I found her in the car three blocks away, crying over the steering wheel because she couldn't find her way home was the first day I was really frightened. And she was frightened, too, for when I tapped on her window, she turned to me and said, "Oh God, what's happening to me? Please help me." A knot twisted in my stomach, but I dared not think the worst.

Six days later the doctor met with her and began a series of tests. I did not understand them then and I do not understand them now, but I suppose it is because I am afraid to know. She spent almost an hour with Dr. Barnwell, and she went back the next day. That day was the longest day I ever spent. I looked through magazines I could not read and played games I did not think about. Finally he called us both into his office and sat us down. She held my arm confidently, but I remember clearly that my own hands were shaking.

"I'm so sorry to have to tell you this," Dr. Barnwell began, "but you seem to be in the early stages of Alzheimer's. . . ."

My mind went blank, and all I could think about was the light that glowed above our heads.

The words echoed in my head: *the early stages of Alzheimer's* . . .

My world spun in circles, and I felt her grip tighten on my arm. She whispered, almost to herself: "Oh, Noah . . . Noah . . ."

And as the tears started to fall, the word came back to me again: . . . *Alzheimer's* . . .

It is a barren disease, as empty and lifeless as a desert. It is a thief of hearts and souls and memories. I did not know what to say to her as she sobbed on my bosom, so I simply held her and rocked her back and forth.

The doctor was grim. He was a good man, and this was hard for him. He was younger than my youngest, and I felt my age in his presence. My mind was confused, my love was shaking, and the only thing I could think was:

> No drowning man can know which drop
> of water his last breath did stop; . . .

A wise poet's words, yet they brought me no comfort. I don't know what they meant or why I thought of them.

We rocked to and fro, and Allie, my dream, my timeless beauty, told me she was sorry. I knew there was nothing to forgive, and I whispered in her ear. "Everything will be fine," I whispered, but inside I was afraid. I was a hollow man with nothing to offer, empty as a junked stovepipe.

I remember only bits and pieces of Dr. Barnwell's continuing explanation.

"It's a degenerative brain disorder affecting memory and personality . . . there is no cure or therapy. . . . There's no way to tell how fast it will progress . . . it differs from person to person. . . . I wish I knew more. . . . Some days will be better than others. . . . It will grow worse with the passage of time. . . . I'm sorry to be the one who has to tell you. . . ."

I'm sorry . . .

I'm sorry . . .

I'm sorry . . .

Everyone was sorry. My children were brokenhearted, my friends were scared for themselves. I don't remember leaving the doctor's office, and I don't remember driving home. My memories of that day are gone, and in this my wife and I are the same.

It has been four years now. Since then we have made the best of it, if that is possible. Allie organized, as was her disposition. She made arrangements to leave the house and move here. She rewrote her will and sealed it. She left specific burial instructions, and they sit in my desk, in the bottom drawer. I have not seen them. And when she was finished, she began to write. Letters to friends and children. Letters to brothers and sisters and cousins. Letters to nieces, nephews, and neighbors. And a letter to me.

I read it sometimes when I am in the mood, and when I do, I am reminded of Allie on cold winter evenings, seated by a roaring fire with a glass of wine at her side, reading the letters I had written to her over the years. She kept them, these letters, and now I keep them, for she made me promise to do so. She said I would know what to do with them. She was right; I find I enjoy reading bits and pieces of them just as she used to. They intrigue me, these letters, for when I sift through them I realize that romance and passion are possible at any age. I see Allie now and know I've never loved her more, but as I read the letters, I come to understand that I have always felt the same way.

I read them last three evenings ago, long after I should have been asleep. It was almost two o'clock when I went to the desk and found the stack of letters, thick and tall and weathered. I untied the ribbon, itself almost half a century old, and found the letters her mother had hidden so long ago and those from afterward. A lifetime of letters, letters professing my love, letters from my heart. I glanced through them with a smile on my face, picking and choosing, and finally opened a letter from our first anniversary.

I read an excerpt:

When I see you now—moving slowly with new life growing inside you—I hope you know how much you mean to me, and how

*special this year has been. No man is more
blessed than me, and I love you with all my
heart.*

I put it aside, sifted through the stack, and
found another, this from a cold evening thirty-
nine years ago.

*Sitting next to you, while our youngest
daughter sang off-key in the school
Christmas show, I looked at you and saw a
pride that comes only to those who feel
deeply in their hearts, and I knew that no
man could be more lucky than me.*

And after our son died, the one who resembled
his mother . . . It was the hardest time we ever
went through, and the words still ring true today:

*In times of grief and sorrow I will hold you
and rock you, and take your grief and
make it my own. When you cry, I cry, and
when you hurt, I hurt. And together we
will try to hold back the floods of tears and
despair and make it through the potholed
streets of life.*

I pause for just a moment, remembering him.
He was four years old at the time, just a baby. I
have lived twenty times as long as he, but if
asked, I would have traded my life for his. It is a

terrible thing to outlive your child, a tragedy I wish upon no one.

I do my best to keep the tears away, sift through some more to clear my mind, and find the next from our twentieth anniversary, something much easier to think about:

> *When I see you, my darling, in the morning before showers or in your studio covered with paint with hair matted and tired eyes, I know that you are the most beautiful woman in the world.*

They went on, this correspondence of life and love, and I read dozens more, some painful, most heartwarming. By three o'clock I was tired, but I had reached the bottom of the stack. There was one letter remaining, the last one I wrote her, and by then I knew I had to keep going.

I lifted the seal and removed both pages. I put the second page aside and moved the first page into better light and began to read:

> *My dearest Allie,*
>
> *The porch is silent except for the sounds that float from the shadows, and for once I am at a loss for words. It is a strange experience for me, for when I think of you and the life we have shared, there is much to remember. A lifetime of memories. But to*

put it into words? I do not know if I am able. I am not a poet, and yet a poem is needed to fully express the way I feel about you.

So my mind drifts, and I remember thinking about our life together as I made coffee this morning. Kate was there, and so was Jane, and they both became quiet when I walked in the kitchen. I saw they'd been crying, and without a word, I sat myself beside them at the table and held their hands. And do you know what I saw when I looked at them? I saw you from so long ago, the day we said good-bye. They resemble you and how you were then, beautiful and sensitive and wounded with the hurt that comes when something special is taken away. And for a reason I'm not sure I understand, I was inspired to tell them a story.

I called Jeff and David into the kitchen, for they were here as well, and when the children were ready, I told them about us and how you came back to me so long ago. I told them about our walk, and the crab dinner in the kitchen, and they listened with smiles when they heard about the canoe ride, and sitting in front of the fire with the storm raging outside. I told them about your mother warning us about Lon the next day—they seemed as surprised as

173

we were—and yes, I even told them what happened later that day, after you went back to town.

That part of the story has never left me, even after all this time. Even though I wasn't there, you described it to me only once, and I remember marveling at the strength you showed that day. I still cannot imagine what was going through your mind when you walked into the lobby and saw Lon, or how it must have felt to talk to him. You told me that the two of you left the inn and sat on a bench by the old Methodist church, and that he held your hand, even as you explained that you must stay.

I know you cared for him. And his reaction proves to me he cared for you as well. No, he could not understand losing you, but how could he? Even as you explained that you had always loved me, and that it wouldn't be fair to him, he did not release your hand. I know he was hurt and angry, and tried for almost an hour to change your mind, but when you stood firm and said, "I can't go back with you, I'm so sorry," he knew that your decision had been made. You said he simply nodded and the two of you sat together for a long time without speaking. I have always wondered what he was thinking as he sat with you, but I'm sure it was the same way I felt only a few hours before. And when he finally walked you to your car, you said he told you that I was a lucky man. He behaved as a gentleman would, and I understood then why your choice was so hard.

I remember that when I finished the story, the room was quiet until Kate finally stood to embrace me. "Oh, Daddy," she said with tears in her eyes, and though I expected to answer their questions, they did not ask any. Instead, they gave me something much more special.

For the next four hours, each of them told me how much we, the two of us, had meant to them growing up. One by one, they told stories about things I had long since forgotten. And by the end, I was crying because I realized how well we had done with raising them. I was so proud of them, and proud of you, and happy about the life we have led. And nothing will ever take that away. Nothing. I only wish you would have been here to enjoy it with me.

After they left, I rocked in silence, thinking back on our life together. You are always here with me when I do so, at least in my heart, and it is impossible for me to remember a time when you were not a part of me. I do not know who I would have become had you never come back to me that day, but I have no doubt that I would have lived and died with regrets that thankfully I'll never know.

I love you, Allie. I am who I am because of you. You are every reason, every hope, and every dream I've ever had, and no matter what happens to us in the future, every day we are together is the greatest day of my life. I will always be yours.

And, my darling, you will always be mine.

Noah

I put the pages aside and remember sitting with Allie on our porch when she read this letter for the first time. It was late afternoon, with red streaks cutting the summer sky, and the last remnants of the day were fading. The sky was slowly changing color, and as I was watching the sun go down, I remember thinking about that brief, flickering moment when day suddenly turns into night.

Dusk, I realized then, is just an illusion, because the sun is either above the horizon or below it. And that means that day and night are linked in a way that few things are; there cannot be one without the other, yet they cannot exist at the same time. How would it feel, I remember wondering, to be always together, yet forever apart?

Looking back, I find it ironic that she chose to

read the letter at the exact moment that question popped into my head. It is ironic, of course, because I know the answer now. I know what it's like to be day and night now; always together, forever apart.

There is beauty where we sit this afternoon, Allie and I. This is the pinnacle of my life. They are here at the creek: the birds, the geese, my friends. Their bodies float on the cool water, which reflects bits and pieces of their colors and make them seem larger than they really are. Allie too is taken in by their wonder, and little by little we get to know each other again.

"It's good to talk to you. I find that I miss it, even when it hasn't been that long."

I am sincere and she knows this, but she is still wary. I am a stranger.

"Is this something we do often?" she asks. "Do we sit here and watch the birds a lot? I mean, do we know each other well?"

"Yes and no. I think everyone has secrets, but we have been acquainted for years."

She looks to her hands, then mine. She thinks about this for a moment, her face at such an angle that she looks young again. We do not wear our rings. Again, there is a reason for this. She asks:

"Were you ever married?"

I nod.

"Yes."

"What was she like?"

I tell the truth.

"She was my dream. She made me who I am, and holding her in my arms was more natural to me than my own heartbeat. I think about her all the time. Even now, when I'm sitting here, I think about her. There could never have been another."

She takes this in. I don't know how she feels about this. Finally she speaks softly, her voice angelic, sensual. I wonder if she knows I think these things.

"Is she dead?"

What is death? I wonder, but I do not say this. Instead I answer, "My wife is alive in my heart. And she always will be."

"You still love her, don't you?"

"Of course. But I love many things. I love to sit here with you. I love to share the beauty of this place with someone I care about. I love to watch the osprey swoop toward the creek and find its dinner."

She is quiet for a moment. She looks away so I can't see her face. It has been her habit for years.

"Why are you doing this?" No fear, just curiosity. This is good. I know what she means, but I ask anyway.

"What?"

"Why are you spending the day with me?"

I smile.

"I'm here because this is where I'm supposed to be. It's not complicated. Both you and I are enjoying ourselves. Don't dismiss my time with you—it's not wasted. It's what I want. I sit here and we talk and I think to myself, What could be better than what I am doing now?"

She looks me in the eyes, and for a moment, just a moment, her eyes twinkle. A slight smile forms on her lips.

"I like being with you, but if getting me intrigued is what you're after, you've succeeded. I admit I enjoy your company, but I know nothing about you. I don't expect you to tell me your life story, but why are you so mysterious?"

"I read once that women love mysterious strangers."

"See, you haven't really answered the question. You haven't answered most of my questions. You didn't even tell me how the story ended this morning."

I shrug. We sit quietly for a while. Finally I ask:

"Is it true?"

"Is what true?"

"That women love mysterious strangers?"

She thinks about this and laughs. Then she answers as I would:

"I think some women do."

"Do you?"

"Now don't go putting me on the spot. I don't know you well enough for that." She is teasing me, and I enjoy it.

We sit silently and watch the world around us. This has taken us a lifetime to learn. It seems only the old are able to sit next to one another and not say anything and still feel content. The young, brash and impatient, must always break the silence. It is a waste, for silence is pure. Silence is holy. It draws people together because only those who are comfortable with each other can sit without speaking. This is the great paradox.

Time passes, and gradually our breathing begins to coincide just as it did this morning. Deep breaths, relaxed breaths, and there is a moment when she dozes off, like those comfortable with one another often do. I wonder if the young are capable of enjoying this. Finally, when she wakes, a miracle.

"Do you see that bird?" She points to it, and I strain my eyes. It is a wonder I can see it, but I can because the sun is bright. I point, too.

"Caspian stern," I say softly, and we devote our attention to it and stare as it glides over Brices Creek. And, like an old habit rediscovered, when I lower my arm, I put my hand on her knee and she doesn't make me move it.

She is right about my evasiveness. On days like these, when only her memory is gone, I am vague in my answers because I've hurt my wife unintentionally with careless slips of my tongue many times these past few years, and I am determined not to let it happen again. So I limit myself and answer only what is asked, sometimes not too well, and I volunteer nothing.

This is a split decision, both good and bad, but necessary, for with knowledge comes pain. To limit the pain I limit my answers. There are days she never learns of her children or that we are married. I am sorry for this, but I will not change.

Does this make me dishonest? Perhaps, but I have seen her crushed by the waterfall of information that is her life. Could I look myself in the mirror without red eyes and quivering jaw and know I have forgotten all that was important to me? I could not and neither can she, for when this odyssey began, this is how I began. Her life, her marriage, her children. Her friends and her work. Questions and answers in the game show format of *This Is Your Life*.

The days were hard on both of us. I was an encyclopedia, an object without feeling, of the whos, whats and wheres in her life, when in reality it is the whys, the things I did not know and could not answer, that make it all worthwhile. She would stare at pictures of forgotten offspring, hold paintbrushes that inspired nothing, and read love letters that brought back no joy. She would weaken over the hours, growing paler, becoming bitter, and ending the day worse than when it began. Our days were lost, and so was she. And selfishly, so was I.

So I changed. I became Magellan or Columbus, an explorer in the mysteries of the mind, and I learned, bumbling and slow, but learning nonetheless what had to be done. And I learned what is obvious to a child. That life is simply a collection of little lives, each lived one day at a time. That each day should be spent finding beauty in flowers and poetry and talking to animals. That a day spent with dreaming and sunsets and refreshing breezes cannot be bettered. But most of all, I learned that life is about sitting on benches next to ancient creeks with my hand on her knee and sometimes, on good days, for falling in love.

"What are you thinking?" she asks.

It is now dusk. We have left our bench and are shuffling along lighted paths that wind their way around this complex. She is holding my arm, and I am her escort. It is her idea to do this. Perhaps she is charmed by me. Perhaps she wants to keep me from falling. Either way, I am smiling to myself.

"I'm thinking about you."

She makes no response to this except to squeeze my arm, and I can tell she likes what I said. Our life together has enabled me to see the clues, even if she does not know them herself. I go on:

"I know you can't remember who you are, but I can, and I find that when I look at you, it makes me feel good."

She taps my arm and smiles. "You're a kind man with a loving heart. I hope I enjoyed you as much before as I do now."

We walk some more. Finally she says, "I have to tell you something."

"Go ahead."

"I think I have an admirer."

"An admirer?"

"Yes."

"I see."

"You don't believe me?"

"I believe you."

"You should."

"Why?"

"Because I think it is you."

I think about this as we walk in silence, holding each other, past the rooms, past the courtyard. We come to the garden, mainly wildflowers, and I stop her. I pick a bundle—red, pink, yellow, violet. I give them to her, and she brings them to her nose. She smells them with eyes closed and she whispers, "They're beautiful." We resume our walk, me in one hand, the flowers in another. People watch us, for we are a walking miracle, or so I am told. It is true in a way, though most times I do not feel lucky.

"You think it's me?" I finally ask.

"Yes."

"Why?"

"Because I have found what you have hidden."

"What?"

"This," she says, handing a small slip of paper to me. "I found it under my pillow."

I read it, and it says:

The body slows with mortal ache, yet my
   promise
remains true at the closing of our days,
A tender touch that ends with a kiss
will awaken love in joyous ways.

"Are there more?" I ask.

"I found this in the pocket of my coat."

Our souls were one, if you must know
and never shall they be apart;
With splendid dawn, your face aglow
I reach for you and find my heart.

"I see," and that is all I say.

We walk as the sun sinks lower in the sky. In time, silver twilight is the only remainder of the day, and still we talk of the poetry. She is enthralled by the romance.

By the time we reach the doorway, I am tired. She knows this, so she stops me with her hand and makes me face her. I do and I realize how hunched over I have become. She and I are now level. Sometimes I am glad she doesn't know how much I have changed. She turns to me and stares for a long time.

"What are you doing?" I ask.

"I don't want to forget you or this day, and I'm trying to keep your memory alive."

Will it work this time? I wonder, then know it will not. It can't. I do not tell her my thoughts, though. I smile instead because her words are sweet.

"Thank you," I say.

"I mean it. I don't want to forget you again. You're very special to me. I don't know what I would have done without you today."

My throat closes a little. There is emotion behind her words, the emotions I feel whenever I think of her. I know this is why I live, and I love her dearly at this moment. How I wish I were strong enough to carry her in my arms to paradise.

"Don't try to say anything," she tells me. "Let's just feel the moment."

And I do, and I feel heaven.

Her disease is worse now than it was in the beginning, though Allie is different from most. There are three others with the disease here, and these three are the sum of my practical experience with it. They, unlike Allie, are in the most advanced stages of Alzheimer's and are almost completely lost. They wake up hallucinating and confused. They repeat themselves over and over. Two of the three can't feed themselves and will die soon. The third has a tendency to wander and get lost. She was found once in a stranger's car a quarter mile away. Since then she has been strapped to the bed. All can be very bitter at times, and at other times they can be like lost children, sad and alone. Seldom do they recognize the staff or people who love them. It is a trying disease, and this is why it is hard for their children and mine to visit.

Allie, of course, has her own problems, too, problems that will probably grow worse over time. She is terribly afraid in the mornings and cries inconsolably. She sees tiny people, like gnomes, I think, watching her, and she screams at them to get away. She bathes willingly but will not eat regularly. She is thin now, much too thin, in my opinion, and on good days I do my best to fatten her up.

But this is where the similarity ends. This is why Allie is considered a miracle, because sometimes, just sometimes, after I read to her, her condition isn't so bad. There is no explanation for this. "It's impossible," the doctors say. "She must not have Alzheimer's." But she does. On most days and every morning there can be no doubt. On this there is agreement.

But why, then, is her condition different? Why does she sometimes change after I read? I tell the doctors the reason—I know it in my heart, but I am not believed. Instead they look to science. Four times specialists have traveled from Chapel Hill to find the answer. Four times they have left without understanding. I tell them, "You can't possibly understand it if you use only your training and your books," but they shake their heads and answer: "Alzheimer's does not work like this. With her condition, it's just not possible to have a conversation or improve as the day goes on. Ever."

But she does. Not every day, not most of the time, and definitely less than she used to. But sometimes. And all that is gone on these days is her memory, as if she has amnesia. But her emotions are normal, her thoughts are normal. And these are the days that I know I am doing right.

Dinner is waiting in her room when we return. It has been arranged for us to eat here, as it always is on days like these, and once again I could ask for no more. The people here take care of everything. They are good to me, and I am thankful.

The lights are dimmed, the room is lit by two candles on the table where we will sit, and music is playing softly in the background. The cups and plates are plastic, and the carafe is filled with apple juice, but rules are rules and she doesn't seem to care. She inhales slightly at the sight. Her eyes are wide.

"Did you do this?"

I nod and she walks in the room.

"It looks beautiful."

I offer my arm in escort and lead her to the window. She doesn't release it when we get there.

187

Her touch is nice, and we stand close together on this crystal springtime evening. The window is open slightly, and I feel a breeze as it fans my cheek. The moon has risen, and we watch for a long time as the evening sky unfolds.

"I've never seen anything so beautiful, I'm sure of it," she says, and I agree with her.

"I haven't, either," I say, but I am looking at her. She knows what I mean, and I see her smile. A moment later she whispers:

"I think I know who Allie went with at the end of the story," she says.

"You do?"

"Yes."

"Who?"

"She went with Noah."

"You're sure?"

"Absolutely."

I smile and nod. "Yes, she did," I say softly, and she smiles back. Her face is radiant.

I pull out her chair with some effort. She sits and I sit opposite her. She offers her hand across the table, and I take it in mine, and I feel her thumb begin to move as it did so many years ago. Without speaking, I stare at her for a long time, living and reliving the moments of my life, remembering it all and making it real. I feel my throat begin to tighten, and once again I realize how much I love her. My voice is shaky when I finally speak.

"You're so beautiful," I say. I can see in her

eyes that she knows how I feel about her and what I really mean by my words.

She does not respond. Instead she lowers her eyes and I wonder what she's thinking. She gives me no clues, and I gently squeeze her hand. I wait. With all my dreams, I know her heart, and I know I'm almost there.

And then, a miracle that proves me right.

As Glenn Miller plays softly in a candlelit room, I watch as she gradually gives in to the feelings inside her. I see a warm smile begin to form on her lips, the kind that makes it all worthwhile, and I watch as she raises her hazy eyes to mine. She pulls my hand toward her.

"You're wonderful. . . ," she says softly, trailing off, and at that moment she falls in love with me, too; this I know, for I have seen the signs a thousand times.

She says nothing else right away, she doesn't have to, and she gives me a look from another lifetime that makes me whole again. I smile back, with as much passion as I can muster, and we stare at each other with the feelings inside us rolling like ocean waves. I look around the room, then up to the ceiling, then back at Allie, and the way she's looking at me makes me warm. And suddenly I feel young again. I'm no longer cold or aching, or hunched over or deformed, or almost blind with cataractal eyes.

I'm strong and proud, and the luckiest man

alive, and I keep on feeling that way for a long time across the table.

By the time the candles have burned down a third, I am ready to break the silence. I say, "I love you deeply, and I hope you know that."

"Of course I do," she says breathlessly. "I've always loved you, Noah."

Noah, I hear again. *Noah.* The word echoes in my head. *Noah . . . Noah.* She knows, I think to myself, she knows who I am. . . .

She knows. . . .

Such a tiny thing, this knowledge, but for me it is a gift from God, and I feel our lifetime together, holding her, loving her, and being with her through the best years of my life.

She murmurs, "Noah . . . my sweet Noah . . ."

And I, who could not accept the doctor's words, have triumphed again, at least for a moment. I give up the pretense of mystery, and I kiss her hand and bring it to my cheek and whisper in her ear. I say:

"You are the greatest thing that has ever happened to me."

"Oh . . . Noah," she says with tears in her eyes, "I love you, too."

If only it would end like this, I would be a happy man.

But it won't. Of this I'm sure, for as time slips by, I begin to see the signs of concern in her face.

"What's wrong?" I ask, and her answer comes softly.

"I'm so afraid. I'm afraid of forgetting you again. It isn't fair . . . I just can't bear to give this up."

Her voice breaks as she finishes, but I don't know what to say. I know the evening is coming to an end, and there is nothing I can do to stop the inevitable. In this I am a failure. I finally tell her:

"I'll never leave you. What we have is forever."

She knows this is all I can do, for neither of us wants empty promises. But I can tell by the way she is looking at me that once again she wishes there were more.

The crickets serenade us, and we begin to pick at our dinner. Neither one of us is hungry, but I lead by example and she follows me. She takes small bites and chews a long time, but I am glad to see her eat. She has lost too much weight in the past three months.

After dinner, I become afraid despite myself. I know I should be joyous, for this reunion is the proof that love can still be ours, but I know the bell has tolled this evening. The sun has long since set and the thief is about to come, and there is nothing I can do to stop it. So I stare at her and wait and live a lifetime in these last remaining moments.

Nothing.

The clock ticks.

Nothing.

I take her in my arms and we hold each other.

Nothing.

I feel her tremble and I whisper in her ear.

Nothing.

I tell her for the last time this evening that I love her.

And the thief comes.

It always amazes me how quickly it happens. Even now, after all this time. For as she holds me, she begins to blink rapidly and shake her head. Then, turning toward the corner of the room, she stares for a long time, concern etched on her face.

No! my mind screams. *Not yet! Not now . . . not when we're so close! Not tonight! Any night but tonight. . . . Please!* The words are inside me. *I can't take it again! It isn't fair . . . it isn't fair. . . .*

But once again, it is to no avail.

"Those people," she finally says, pointing, "are staring at me. Please make them stop."

The gnomes.

A pit rises in my stomach, hard and full. My breathing stops for a moment, then starts again, this time shallower. My mouth goes dry, and I feel my heart pounding. It is over, I know, and I am right. The sundowning has come. This, the evening confusion associated with Alzheimer's disease that affects my wife, is the hardest part of all. For when it comes, she is gone, and sometimes I wonder whether she and I will ever love again.

"There's no one there, Allie," I say, trying to fend off the inevitable. She doesn't believe me.

"They're staring at me."

"No," I whisper while shaking my head.

"You can't see them?"

"No," I say, and she thinks for a moment.

"Well, they're right there," she says, pushing me away, "and they're staring at me."

With that, she begins to talk to herself, and moments later, when I try to comfort her, she flinches with wide eyes.

"Who are you?" she cries with panic in her voice, her face becoming whiter. "What are you doing here?" There is fear growing inside her, and I hurt, for there is nothing I can do. She moves farther from me, backing away, her hands in a defensive position, and then she says the most heartbreaking words of all.

"Go away! Stay away from me!" she screams. She is pushing the gnomes away from her, terrified, now oblivious of my presence.

I stand and cross the room to her bed. I am weak now, my legs ache, and there is a strange pain in my side. I don't know where it comes from. It is a struggle to press the button to call the nurses, for my fingers are throbbing and seem frozen together, but I finally succeed. They will be here soon now, I know, and I wait for them. While I wait, I stare at my wife.

Ten . . .

Twenty . . .

Thirty seconds pass, and I continue to stare, my eyes missing nothing, remembering the moments we just shared together. But in all that time she does not look back, and I am haunted by the visions of her struggling with unseen enemies.

I sit by the bedside with an aching back and start to cry as I pick up the notebook. Allie does not notice. I understand, for her mind is gone.

A couple of pages fall to the floor, and I bend over to pick them up. I am tired now, so I sit, alone and apart from my wife. And when the nurses come in they see two people they must comfort. A woman shaking in fear from demons in her mind, and the old man who loves her more deeply than life itself, crying softly in the corner, his face in his hands.

I spend the rest of the evening alone in my room. My door is partially open and I see people walk by, some strangers, some friends, and if I concentrate, I can hear them talking about families, jobs, and visits to parks. Ordinary conversations, nothing more, but I find that I envy them and the ease of their communication. Another deadly sin, I know, but sometimes I can't help it.

Dr. Barnwell is here, too, speaking with one of the nurses, and I wonder who is ill enough to warrant such a visit at this hour. He works too much, I tell him. Spend the time with your family, I say, they won't be around forever. But he doesn't listen to me. He cares for his patients, he says, and must come here when called. He says he has no choice, but this makes him a man torn by contradiction. He wants to be a doctor completely devoted to his patients and a man completely devoted to his family. He cannot be both, for there aren't enough hours, but he has yet to learn this. I wonder, as his voice fades into the background, which he will choose or whether, sadly, the choice will be made for him.

I sit by the window in an easy chair and I think about today. It was happy and sad, wonderful and heart-wrenching. My conflicting emotions keep me silent for many hours. I did not read to anyone this evening; I could not, for poetic introspection would bring me to tears. In time, the hallways become quiet except for the footfalls of evening soldiers. At eleven o'clock I hear the familiar sounds that for some reason I expected. The footsteps I know so well.

Dr. Barnwell peeks in.

"I noticed your light was on. Do you mind if I come in?"

"No," I say, shaking my head.

He comes in and looks around the room before taking a seat a few feet from me.

"I hear," he says, "you had a good day with Allie." He smiles. He is intrigued by us and the

relationship we have. I do not know if his inter-
est is entirely professional.

"I suppose so."

He cocks his head at my answer and looks at
me. "You okay, Noah? You look a little down."

"I'm fine. Just a little tired."

"How was Allie today?"

"She was okay. We talked for almost four
hours."

"Four hours? Noah, that's . . . incredible."

I can only nod. He goes on, shaking his head.

"I've never seen anything like it, or even heard
about it. I guess that's what love is all about. You
two were meant for each other. She must love
you very much. You know that, don't you?"

"I know," I say, but I can't say anything more.

"What's really bothering you, Noah? Did
Allie say or do something that hurt your feelings?"

"No. She was wonderful, actually. It's just
that right now I feel . . . alone."

"Alone?"

"Yes."

"Nobody's alone."

"I'm alone," I say as I look at my watch and
think of his family sleeping in a quiet house, the
place he should be, "and so are you."

The next few days passed without signifi-
cance. Allie was unable to recognize me at any
time, and I admit my attention waned now and

then, for most of my thoughts were of the day we had just spent. Though the end always comes too soon, there was nothing lost that day, only gained, and I was happy to have received this blessing once again.

By the following week, my life had pretty much returned to normal. Or at least as normal as my life can be. Reading to Allie, reading to others, wandering the halls. Lying awake at night and sitting by my heater in the morning. I find a strange comfort in the predictability of my life.

On a cool, foggy morning eight days after she and I had spent our day together, I woke early, as is my custom, and puttered around my desk, alternately looking at photographs and reading letters written many years before. At least I tried to. I couldn't concentrate too well because I had a headache, so I put them aside and went to sit in my chair by the window to watch the sun come up. Allie would be awake in a couple of hours, I knew, and I wanted to be refreshed, for reading all day would only make my head hurt more.

I closed my eyes for a few minutes while my head alternately pounded and subsided. Then, opening them, I watched my old friend, the creek, roll by my window. Unlike Allie, I had been given a room where I could see it, and it has never failed to inspire me. It is a contradiction— this creek—a hundred thousand years old but renewed with each rainfall. I talked to it that morning, whispered so it could hear, "You are blessed, my friend, and I am blessed, and together we meet the coming days." The ripples and waves circled and twisted in agreement, the pale glow of morning light reflecting the world we share. The creek and I. Flowing, ebbing, receding. It is life, I think, to watch the water. A man can learn so many things.

It happened as I sat in the chair, just as the sun first peeked over the horizon. My hand, I noticed, started to tingle, something it had never done before. I started to lift it, but I was forced to stop when my head pounded again, this time hard, almost as if I had been hit in the head with a hammer. I closed my eyes, then squeezed my lids tight. My hand stopped tingling and began to go numb, quickly, as if my nerves were suddenly severed somewhere on my lower arm. My wrist locked as a shooting pain rocked my head and seemed to flow down my neck and into every cell of my body, like a tidal wave, crushing and wasting everything in its path.

I lost my sight, and I heard what sounded like a train roaring inches from my head, and I knew that I was having a stroke. The pain coursed through my body like a lightning bolt, and in my last remaining moments of consciousness, I pictured Allie, lying in her bed, waiting for the story I would never read, lost and confused, completely and totally unable to help herself. Just like me.

And as my eyes closed for the final time, I thought to myself, Oh God, what have I done?

I was unconscious on and off for days, and in those moments when I was awake, I found myself hooked to machines, tubes up my nose and down my throat and two bags of fluid hanging near the bed. I could hear the faint hum of machines, droning on and off, sometimes making sounds I could not recognize. One machine, beeping with my heart rate, was strangely soothing, and I found myself lulled to never-land time and time again.

The doctors were worried. I could see the concern in their faces through squinted eyes as they scanned the charts and adjusted the machines. They whispered their thoughts, thinking I couldn't hear. "Strokes could be serious," they'd say, "especially for someone his age, and the consequences could be severe." Grim faces would prelude their predictions—"loss of speech, loss of movement, paralysis." Another chart notation, another beep of a strange machine, and they'd leave, never knowing I heard every word. I tried not to think of these things afterward but instead concentrated on Allie, bringing a picture of her to my mind whenever I could. I did my best to bring her life into mine, to make us one again. I tried to feel her touch, hear her voice, see her face, and when I did tears would fill my eyes because I didn't know if I would be able to hold her again, to whisper to her, to spend the day with her talking and reading and walking. This was not how I'd imagined, or hoped, it would end. I'd always assumed I would go last. This wasn't how it was supposed to be.

I drifted in and out of consciousness for days until another foggy morning when my promise to Allie spurred my body once again. I opened my eyes and saw a room full of flowers, and their scent motivated me further. I looked for the buzzer, struggled to press it, and a nurse arrived thirty seconds later, followed closely by Dr. Barnwell, who smiled almost immediately.

"I'm thirsty," I said with a raspy voice, and Dr. Barnwell smiled broadly.

"Welcome back," he said, "I knew you'd make it."

Two weeks later I am able to leave the hospital, though I am only half a man now. If I were a Cadillac, I would drive in circles, one wheel turning, for the right side of my body is weaker than the left. This, they tell me, is good news, for the paralysis could have been total. Sometimes, it seems, I am surrounded by optimists.

The bad news is that my hands prevent me from using either cane or wheelchair, so I must now march to my own unique cadence to keep upright. Not left-right-left as was common in my youth, or even the shuffle-shuffle of late, but rather slow-shuffle, slide-the-right, slow-shuffle.

I am an epic adventure now when I travel the halls. It is slow going even for me, this coming from a man who could barely outpace a turtle two weeks ago.

It is late when I return, and when I reach my room, I know I will not sleep. I breathe deeply and smell the springtime fragrances that filter through my room. The window has been left open, and there is a slight chill in the air. I find that I am invigorated by the change in temperature. Evelyn, one of the many nurses here who is one-third my age, helps me to the chair that sits by the window and begins to close it. I stop her, and though her eyebrows rise, she accepts my decision. I hear a drawer open, and a moment later a sweater is draped over my shoulders. She adjusts it as if I were a child, and when she is finished, she puts her hand on my shoulder and pats it gently. She says nothing as she does this, and by her silence I know that she is staring out the window. She does not move for a long time, and I wonder what she is thinking, but I do not ask. Eventually I hear her sigh. She turns to leave, and as she does, she stops, leans forward, and then kisses me on the cheek, tenderly, the way my granddaughter does. I am surprised by this, and she says quietly, "It's good to have you back. Allie's missed you and so have the rest of us. We were all praying for you because it's just not the same around here when you're gone." She smiles at me and touches my face before she leaves. I say nothing. Later I hear her walk by again, pushing a cart, talking to another nurse, their voices hushed.

The stars are out tonight, and the world is glowing an eerie blue. The crickets are singing, and their sound drowns out everything else. As I sit, I wonder if anyone outside can see me, this prisoner of flesh. I search the trees, the court-yard, the benches near the geese, looking for signs of life, but there is nothing. Even the creek is still. In the darkness it looks like empty space, and I find that I'm drawn to its mystery. I watch for hours, and as I do, I see the reflection of clouds as they begin to bounce off the water. A storm is coming, and in time the sky will turn sil-ver, like dusk again.

Lightning cuts the wild sky, and I feel my mind drift back. Who are we, Allie and I? Are we ancient ivy on a cypress tree, tendrils and branches intertwined so closely that we would both die if we were forced apart? I don't know. Another bolt and the table beside me is lit enough to see a picture of Allie, the best one I have. I had it framed years ago in the hope that the glass would make it last forever. I reach for it and hold it inches from my face. I stare at it for a long time, I can't help it. She was forty-one when it was taken, and she had never been more beautiful. There are so many things I want to ask her, but I know the picture won't answer, so I put it aside.

Tonight, with Allie down the hall, I am alone. I will always be alone. This I thought as I lay in the hospital. This I'm sure of as I look out the window and watch the storm clouds appear. Despite myself I am saddened by our plight, for I realize that the last day we were together I never kissed her lips. Perhaps I never will again. It is impossible to tell with this disease. Why do I think such things?

I finally stand and walk to my desk and turn on the lamp. This takes more effort than I think it will, and I am strained, so I do not return to the window seat. I sit down and spend a few minutes looking at the pictures that sit on my desk. Family pictures, pictures of children and vacations. Pictures of Allie and me. I think back to the times we shared together, alone or with family, and once again I realize how ancient I am.

I open a drawer and find the flowers I'd once given her long ago, old and faded and tied together with ribbon. They, like me, are dry and brittle and difficult to handle without breaking. But she saved them. "I don't understand what you want with them," I would say, but she would just ignore me. And sometimes in the evenings I would see her holding them, almost reverently, as if they offered the secret of life itself. Women.

Since this seems to be a night of memories, I look for and find my wedding ring. It is in the top drawer, wrapped in tissue. I cannot wear it anymore because my knuckles are swollen and my fingers lack for blood. I unwrap the tissue and find it unchanged. It is powerful, a symbol, a circle, and I know, *I know,* there could never have been another. I knew it then, and I know it now. And in that moment I whisper aloud, "I am still yours, Allie, my queen, my timeless beauty. You are, and always have been, the best thing in my life."

I wonder if she hears me when I say this, and I wait for a sign. But there is nothing.

It is eleven-thirty and I look for the letter she wrote me, the one I read when the mood strikes me. I find it where I last left it. I turn it over a couple of times before I open it, and when I do my hands begin to tremble. Finally I read:

Dear Noah,

I write this letter by candlelight as you lie sleeping in the bedroom we have shared since the day we were married. And though I can't hear the soft sounds of your slumber, I know you are there, and soon I will be lying next to you again as I always have. And I will feel your warmth and your comfort, and your breaths will slowly guide me to the place where I dream of you and the wonderful man you are.

I see the flame beside me and it reminds

me of another fire from decades ago, with me in your soft clothes and you in your jeans. I knew then we would always be together, even though I wavered the fol- lowing day. My heart had been captured, roped by a southern poet, and I knew inside that it had always been yours. Who was I to question a love that rode on shoot- ing stars and roared like crashing waves? For that is what it was between us then and that is what it is today.

I remember coming back to you the next day, the day my mother visited. I was so scared, more scared than I had ever been because I was sure you would never forgive me for leaving you. I was shaking as I got out of the car, but you took it all away with your smile and the way you held your hand out to me. "How 'bout some coffee," was all you said. And you never brought it up again. In all our years together.

Nor did you question me when I would leave and walk alone the next few days. And when I came in with tears in my eyes, you always knew whether I needed you to hold me or to just let me be. I don't know how you knew, but you did, and you made it easier for me. Later when we went to the small chapel and traded our rings and made our vows, I looked in your eyes and knew I had made the right decision. But more than that, I knew I was foolish for ever considering someone else. I have never wavered since.

We had a wonderful life together, and I think about it a lot now. I close my eyes sometimes and see you with speckles of gray in your hair, sitting on the porch and playing your guitar while little ones play and clap to the music you create. Your clothes are stained from hours of work and you are tired, and though I offer you time to relax, you smile and say, "That's what I am doing now." I find your love for our children very sensual and exciting. "You're a better father than you know," I tell you later, after the children are sleeping. Soon after, we peel off our clothes and kiss each other and almost lose ourselves before we are able to slip between the flannel sheets.

I love you for many things, especially your passions, for they have always been those things which are most beautiful in life. Love and poetry and fatherhood and friendship and beauty and nature. And I am glad you have taught the children these things, for I know their lives are better for it. They tell me how special you are to them, and every time they do, it makes me feel like the luckiest woman alive.

You have taught me as well, and inspired me, and supported me in my painting, and you will never know how much it has meant to me. My works hang in museums and private collections now, and though there have been times when I was frazzled and distracted because of shows and critics, you were always there with kind words, encouraging me. You understood my need for my own studio, my own space, and saw beyond the paint on my clothes and in my hair and sometimes on the furniture. I know it was not easy. It takes a man to do that, Noah, to live with something like that. And you have. For forty-five years now. Wonderful years.

You are my best friend as well as my lover, and I do not know which side of you I enjoy the most. I treasure each side, just as I have treasured our life together. You have something inside you, Noah, something beautiful and strong. Kindness, that's what I see when I look at you now, that's what everyone sees. Kindness. You are the most forgiving and peaceful man I know. God is with you, He must be, for you are the closest thing to an angel that I've ever met.

I know you thought me crazy for making us write our story before we finally leave our home, but I have my reasons and I thank you for your patience. And though you asked, I never told you why, but now I think it is time you knew.

We have lived a lifetime most couples never know, and yet, when I look at you, I am frightened by the knowledge that all this will be ending soon. For we both know my prognosis and what it will mean to us. I see your tears and I worry more about you than I do about me, because I fear the pain I know you will go through. There are no words to express my sorrow for this, and I am at a loss for words.

So I love you so deeply, so incredibly much, that I will find a way to come back to you despite my disease, I promise you that. And this is where the story comes in. When I am lost and lonely, read this story—just as you told it to the children— and know that in some way, I will realize it's about us. And perhaps, just perhaps, we will find a way to be together again.

Please don't be angry with me on days I do not remember you, and we both know they will come. Know that I love you, that I always will, and that no matter what happens, know I have led the greatest life possible. My life with you.

And if you save this letter to read again, then believe what I am writing for you now. Noah, wherever you are and whenever this is, I love you. I love you now as I write this, and I love you now as you read this. And I am so sorry if I am not able to

tell you. I love you deeply, my husband.
You are, and always have been, my dream.

Allie

When I am finished with the letter, I put it
aside. I rise from my desk and find my slippers.
They are near my bed, and I must sit to put them
on. Then, standing, I cross the room and open
my door. I peek down the hall and see Janice
seated at the main desk. At least I think it is
Janice. I must pass this desk to get to Allie's
room, but at this hour I am not supposed to
leave my room, and Janice has never been one to
bend the rules. Her husband is a lawyer.

I wait to see if she will leave, but she does not
seem to be moving, and I grow impatient. I finally
exit my room anyway, slow-shuffle, slide-the-right,
slow-shuffle. It takes aeons to close the distance,
but for some reason she does not see me approach-
ing. I am a silent panther creeping through the jun-
gle, I am as invisible as baby pigeons.

In the end I am discovered, but I am not surprised. I stand before her.

"Noah," she says, "what are you doing?"

"I'm taking a walk," I say. "I can't sleep."

"You know you're not supposed to do this."

"I know."

I don't move, though. I am determined.

"You're not really going for a walk, are you?
You're going to see Allie."

"Yes," I answer.

"Noah, you know what happened the last time you saw her at night."

"I remember."

"Then you know you shouldn't be doing this."

I don't answer directly. Instead I say, "I miss her."

"I know you do, but I can't let you see her."

"It's our anniversary," I say. This is true. It is one year before gold. Forty-nine years today.

"I see."

"Then I can go?"

She looks away for a moment, and her voice changes. Her voice is softer now, and I am surprised. She has never struck me as the sentimental type.

"Noah, I've worked here for five years and I worked at another home before that. I've seen hundreds of couples struggle with grief and sadness, but I've never seen anyone handle it like you do. No one around here, not the doctors, not the nurses, has ever seen anything like it."

She pauses for just a moment, and strangely, her eyes begin to fill with tears. She wipes them with her finger and goes on:

"I try to think what it's like for you, how you keep going day after day, but I can't even imagine it. I don't know how you do it. You even beat her disease sometimes. Even though the doctors don't understand it, we nurses do. It's love, it's as simple as that. It's the most incredible thing I've ever seen."

A lump has risen in my throat, and I am speechless.

"But Noah, you're not supposed to do this, and I can't let you. So go back to your room." Then, smiling softly and sniffling and shuffling some papers on the desk, she says: "Me, I'm going downstairs for some coffee. I won't be back to check on you for a while, so don't do anything foolish."

She rises quickly, touches my arm, and walks toward the stairs. She doesn't look back, and suddenly I am alone. I don't know what to think. I look at where she had been sitting and see her coffee, a full cup, still steaming, and once again I learn that there are good people in the world.

I am warm for the first time in years as I begin my trek to Allie's room. I take steps the size of Pixie straws, and even at that pace it is dangerous, for my legs have grown tired already. I find I must touch the wall to keep from falling down. Lights buzz overhead, their fluorescent glow making my eyes ache, and I squint a little. I walk by a dozen darkened rooms, rooms where I have read before, and I realize I miss the people inside. They are my friends, whose faces I know so well, and I will see them all tomorrow. But not tonight, for there is no time to stop on this journey. I press on, and the movement forces blood through banished arteries. I feel myself becoming stronger with every step. I hear a door open behind me, but I don't hear footsteps, and I keep going. I am a stranger now. I cannot be stopped. A phone rings in the nurses' station, and I push forward so I will not be caught. I am a midnight bandit, masked and fleeing on horseback from sleepy desert towns, charging into yellow moons with gold dust in my saddlebags. I am young and strong with passion in my heart, and I will break down the door and lift her in my arms and carry her to paradise.

Who am I kidding?

I lead a simple life now. I am foolish, an old man in love, a dreamer who dreams of nothing but reading to Allie and holding her whenever I can. I am a sinner with many faults and a man who believes in magic, but I am too old to change and too old to care.

When I finally reach her room my body is weak. My legs wobble, my eyes are blurred, and my heart is beating funny inside my chest. I struggle with the knob, and in the end it takes two hands and three truckloads of effort. The door opens and light from the hallway spills in, illuminating the bed where she sleeps. I think, as I see her, I am nothing but a passerby on a busy city street, forgotten forever.

Her room is quiet, and she is lying with the covers halfway up. After a moment I see her roll to one side, and her noises bring back memories of happier times. She looks small in her bed, and as I watch her I know it is over between us. The air is stale and I shiver. This place has become our tomb.

I do not move, on this our anniversary, for almost a minute, and I long to tell her how I feel, but I stay quiet so I won't wake her. Besides, it is written on the slip of paper that I will slide under her pillow. It says:

Love, in these last and tender hours
is sensitive and very pure
Come morning light with soft-lit powers
to awaken love that's ever sure.

I think I hear someone coming, so I enter her room and close the door behind me. Blackness descends and I cross her floor from memory and reach the window. I open the curtains, and the moon stares back, large and full, the guardian of the evening. I turn to Allie and dream a thousand dreams, and though I know I should not, I sit on her bed while I slip the note beneath her pillow. Then I reach across and gently touch her face, soft like powder. I stroke her hair, and my breath is taken away. I feel wonder, I feel awe, like a composer first discovering the works of Mozart. She stirs and opens her eyes, squinting softly, and I suddenly regret my foolishness, for I know she will begin to cry and scream, for this is what she always does. I am impulsive and weak, this I know, but I feel an urge to attempt the impossible and I lean toward her, our faces drawing closer.

And when her lips meet mine, I feel a strange tingling I have never felt before, in all our years together, but I do not pull back. And suddenly, a miracle, for I feel her mouth open and I discover a forgotten paradise, unchanged all this time, ageless like the stars. I feel the warmth of her body, and as our tongues meet, I allow myself to slip away, as I had so many years ago. I close my eyes and become a mighty ship in churning waters, strong and fearless, and she is my sails. I gently trace the outline of her cheek, then take her hand in mine. I kiss her lips, her cheeks, and listen as she takes a breath. She murmurs softly, "Oh, Noah . . . I've missed you." Another miracle—the greatest of all!—and there's no way I can stop the tears as we begin to slip toward heaven itself. For at that moment, the world is full of wonder as I feel her fingers reach for the buttons on my shirt and slowly, ever so slowly, she begins to undo them one by one.